THUNDER PASS

**Center Point
Large Print**

**This Large Print Book carries the
Seal of Approval of N.A.V.H.**

ॐ श्री गणेशाय नमः

LAURAN PAINE

THUNDER PASS

CENTER POINT PUBLISHING

THORNDIKE, MAINE

This Center Point Large Print edition
is published in the year 2003 by arrangement with
Golden West Literary Agency.

The text of this Large Print edition is unabridged. In other
aspects, this book may vary from the original edition. Printed in
Thailand. Set in 16-point Times New Roman type by
Bill Coskrey and Gary Socquet.

ISBN 1-58547-266-2

Library of Congress Cataloging-in-Publication Data.

Paine, Lauran.
    Thunder Pass / Lauran Paine.--Center Point large print ed.
        p. cm.
    ISBN 1-58547-266-2 (lib. bdg. : alk. paper)
    1. Large type books. I. Title.

PS3566.A34 T47 2003
813'.54--dc21

                                                        2002073919

THUNDER PASS

CHAPTER ONE

SHE stood in the sweltering shade of the transport company's warped wooden overhang with her parasol tilted against the gelatin glare arising from mustard-coloured earth and beating downward from a steely sky, and kept her level gaze northward for sight of a buggy or even a band of riders loping up with an extra horse, but neither of these things appeared.

A pulsing haze hung over the far distances and over by Thunder Pass, the main route into Lincoln Valley, there lay a bitter iridescence. Mid-summer in Oklahoma was a sizzling period of lassitude and short-tempers. It was also a time for the Texas drives to pass through north-bound for the Kansas Plains. Finally, it had up until this year been the time for Kathy Merritt to return home for that blissful rest after the final spring semester of school.

But this year was different; she had returned home as always after the ceremonies, only this year she had graduated. She would not be going back down to San Antonio again. She was no longer, in the eyes of the academic authorities, a schoolgirl. She was a woman now with all the poise and education *Mrs. Heppelwhite's Academy for Young Ladies* could instil in her.

She was a slim, long-legged girl and carried the unmistakable mark of a proud line. Her eyes were a peculiar gold-flecked shade of light grey and the lashes around them were black. Her hair was also black but her flesh was creamy, which made quite a contrast and in San

Antonio men had readily noticed her. They'd noticed her also in her home town where she now stood impatiently waiting; in fact men noticed Kathy Merritt wherever she was.

She was full at breast and hip with a long, heavy mouth. There was a squareness to her jaw that gave it perfect balance—and also gave it unmistakable strength. She showed a strong-willed competence not uncommon on the frontier, and although her modish clothing and little parasol were out of place at Thunder City, she looked quite at home.

Now, her skin was flushed from the steady mid-summer heat and also from annoyance. She had written her father three weeks earlier when she'd arrive in Thunder City but now that she was here there was no buggy waiting, not even a saddlehorse.

Chester Peters, the stageline clerk, walked on out with his clipboard and his green eyeshade and his elegant sleeve-garters, squinted northward and cleared his throat apologetically as though this was all his fault, which of course it wasn't.

"Expect somethin' come up," he suggested mildly, watching her face, her rock-set profile, in a sidelong way. Chester knew these Merritts. There was only Kathy now and her father. Once there had been two brothers and their mother, but Jared Merritt's wife had been taken off by the typhoid and his two sons had died in the war—one in Yankee blue, one in Secesh grey.

But the iron was still there in the girl and also in her tough old father. Adversity changed these people like it invariably changed everyone else, but with these Merritts it left lines, and shades of pain in the eyes, but it couldn't touch that inbred iron.

"If you'd like I'll fetch you a glass of lemonade an' you can drink it inside, Miss Kathy, for it's fair-hot out here even in the shade. My weather-glass says a hundred-sixteen."

She turned, showing old Chester a too-sweet smile with her lilting lips; showing him too a steady flame in the depths of her startlingly light grey eyes surrounded as they were by those thick black lashes. Firepoints danced in those eyes but when she spoke her voice was soft and feminine because she'd learned her lessons well at Mrs. Heppelwhite's school.

"Thank you, Chester, but I'm not thirsty. I'll wait out here."

"As you wish," he mumbled, touched his eyeshade and stepped around her to the very edge of the plankwalk where he consulted a large gold watch and also consulted the southward shimmering run of withered countryside for the noon stage, which he did not see.

Across the road a bronzed man wearing a black hat and an ivory-butted .45 lashed to his right leg sauntered along. He was a stranger to Kathy Merritt but when he glanced over, saw her gazing at him, he made a graceful little bow and brushed the rim of his black hat with long fingers. He was wearing a badge upon his shirtfront.

She said, "Chester; what happened to Marshal Clampett?"

Chester looked at that sauntering, tall man for a quiet moment before he said, "Well, Miss Kathy, Marshal

Clampett got pretty old for that kind of work."

"Oh. Father didn't mention in his letters that the Marshal had retired."

"Well Miss Kathy, he didn't retire—exactly." Chester's head gradually turned as his eyes followed that lanky sauntering man on across the shimmering roadway. "He got killed. That's what I meant about him gettin' kind of old for his line of work. A man hits forty, ma'am, his best years are behind him in a lot of ways."

Death always has its sobering impact even when it strikes strangers, but when it reaches out for someone remembered and liked, it can turn a person's entire train of thought away from other things. Kathy stood there looking up where that bronzed man was strolling through layers of heat, thinking not of him at all, but of that badge he wore and the weathered, smiling, quiet-spoken man who had worn it before. Who had worn it in fact since she'd been a stub-nosed, freckle-faced gangling girl in jeans and pigtails.

Marshal Clampett had seemed as permanent in her world as Oklahoma's red dust or its pitiless summertime sun. He'd come by Thunder Pass Ranch burnt berry-brown by summer suns and wrapped like a big bear in his wintertime sheepskins. He'd always had a twinkle for her and a laugh. They had shared confidences and the last time she'd taken the coach out, he'd been there to pull upon his grey moustache and regard her with that solicitude of an older man interested in a lone girl's welfare, and also with the admiring sparkle of a man still youthful enough to appreciate genuine beauty.

Now he was dead.

Two Indians came riding into town from the east, both of them beggarly in appearance, both of them wearing greasy blankets in spite of the merciless, breathless heat. Their veiled black eyes swung off towards that lanky man with the badge, lingered a moment, then swung on over where Kathy stood back a few feet in the useless shade. All this Oklahoma country had once been Indian Territory, so named and so administered, for it had been here, northward of the Texas Panhandle, that the government had been shipping its redskin wards—and nuisances—for nearly a hundred years. The inevitable result was that a heterogeneous mixture now lived here on the fringes of the civilised world, actually little different now from earlier times, sometimes indifferent, sometimes violent. Even those like Kathy's father who had fought and councilled and lived with these people could not accurately predict their moods or their thoughts. In their own world they were aliens, but they had to be tolerated. They were here by the thousands, lice-infested, uncommunicative, alternately apathetic and wildly explosive, but they were here.

Chester viewed those two slouched scarecrows when they poked on past atop their emaciated, scabby horses with an expression of sniffing distaste. He said nothing about them but he didn't have to, his posture said enough.

Kathy was put in mind of old Miranda, the Choctaw squaw her father had brought to Thunder Pass Ranch after the death of her mother. Miranda was intended for the substitute she could never be and never was, but she had been a female in that otherwise masculine world of Thunder Pass Ranch, and over the years they had come to share a bond of affection. Old Miranda used to bristle and push her short, stout body forward when one of the cowboys would smile at Kathy or show her their wicked smiles. Old Miranda knew men, and in her own private jargon which was part Choctaw, part bad English and worse Spanish, she told Kathy in bitter tones that men were no good; that they were fit only for hunting and warring and loafing.

It had taken four years for Kathy to conceal adequately much that had become part of her through those formative years at Thunder Pass Ranch. As a matter of fact her first semester at Mrs. Heppelwhite's school had nearly also been her last. She couldn't now recall exactly what had sparked it, but in a moment of anger she had stunned her classmates once by a sizzling string of epithets in Miranda's jargon. It had afterwards taken considerable contrition to persuade Mrs. Heppelwhite not to send her bag and baggage back to Oklahoma.

But a girl learned, if she had the Merritt will and the Merritt iron; she learned all the outward manifestations of ladylike behaviour, acquired the long-legged poise which was now so much a part of her, and yet she never forgot the other things either, for the powerful forces of environment leave their eternal marks in the mind, upon the soul, and even in the heart.

Chester turned, his smile long and soft. "There's dust on the northward trace," he said. "It'll be your paw and a rig coming, Miss Kathy."

She saw that dust too but she had better eyesight. "Riders," she stated, "not a rig," and bit her underlip in vexation. She wasn't dressed for straddling a horse.

"Well no ma'am, if you'd like I'd be right proud to trot on over to the liverybarn and fetch you back a buggy."

She declined this offer and steadily watched that yonder dust jump into the motionless atmosphere and hang there. Farther back, soft-hazed in the dancing heat, lay the Thunder Mountains. They were blue-tiered with stiff-topped trees and their fleshy shoulders showed softly round and solid. Below them where the land began its gentle rise upwards that wide notch which was Thunder Pass, lay the ranch. Eastward as well as southward and westward ran the thousands of summer-cured grassy acres. A little pang of inexplicable sadness touched her heart; it was a pain she couldn't define. It was part anticipation, part regret for a closed chapter in her life, part sadness that the years were marching unalterably onward.

Miranda wouldn't be changed much; a little fatter and squattier, a little quieter perhaps. Indians never seemed to age. Her father would be nearly white-haired by now. Last year she'd seen the signs. And he'd be less erect, less spry probably, because the last time he'd brought her down to Thunder City to catch the south-bound coach he'd brought along the wrangler to wrestle her baggage, something he'd never done before.

But these were things she could only guess at because her father was not an outstanding correspondent. He'd written her exactly two letters this last semester, and

Miranda couldn't write at all. Of course there was their rangeboss, even-tempered and kindly Jack Carson, but Jack had written her just one letter in four years although he'd solemnly promised to do better the last time she'd seen him. The trouble was, Jack was somewhere between her father and Miranda as a letter-writer; he wasn't exactly illiterate, but he was close enough to it to be conscious of this painful shortcoming when he knew she would be conscious of it too, so in the end he'd kept his word, after a fashion, by not writing but by not quite breaking his word either. He'd buy newspapers, use his Barlow knife to cut out articles he thought would interest her, stuff them into a smudged envelope and mail them to her.

The dust banner came closer. There were visible men beneath it now, tiny and bunched up as they swept along. She strained to make out some of those men, Jack perhaps and her father, one or two of the other men who'd been on Thunder Pass Ranch down the years. They came and they went, those Oklahoma cowboys, but there was the same oldtime nucleus, some as grey as her father, who'd been content to stay. They were her family and as she strained ahead to recognise them her eyes suddenly burned with a peculiar wet hotness. Home again, this time for good. Tomorrow she would carefully put away the modish dresses and the perky little hats, the velvet choker and the parasol. Tomorrow she would open a fresh page in her life. Tomorrow she would listen to her father and to Miranda, catch up on all the news. She would ride her chestnut mare and feel hot sunlight on bare throat and arms.

CHAPTER TWO

THOSE riders slacked off at the edge of town and walked their sweat-shiny mounts on down the empty roadway with alkali dust lying powder-fine upon them. She saw Jack Carson slightly ahead, his face as darkly layered by suntan as always, his cheekbones high and flat-planed beneath level faded eyes, his long mouth gravely flattened as though with disapproval. He didn't look quite as she'd remembered him but it wasn't a difference she could define.

He reined on over and touched his hatbrim, his gaze downward at her warm and yet also oddly reserved.

The four riders with Carson were all strangers to her. They were young men, leaned-down from a raw environment and hard work, bronzed and capable-looking. They seemed very similar in most things, in their bold gazes, in the way they wore their tied-down forty-fives, in the easy, confident way they sat their saddles. Too much alike, she thought, as she smiled up at Jack Carson, too confident, too challenging.

"How are you, Jack?"

He said, "Fine, Kathy, and you're lookin' right well." He closed his lips and continued to quietly regard her with that odd, reserved expression for a moment, then he said, "Your paw wasn't able to make it. Nothin' serious, just a lot of things that'll keep him on the ranch for a spell." Carson looked downwards and upwards. "Reckon we'll have to get you a livery rig, you can't hardly ride back dressed like that."

He rolled his head towards one of the bold-eyed cowboys to speak, but she headed that off. "Never mind. I'll change at the hotel and ride that extra horse you brought along. I'll only be a minute."

She moved off southward two doors towards the hotel. As she stepped on into the gloomy little lobby she saw that lanky man with the black hat and Marshal Clampett's badge standing with his hands behind him looking out the window up where Carson and his Thunder Pass men were sitting their horses. He turned slowly to show her a solemn, handsome face full of marked interest in her and masculine curiosity. She went on past, asked the desk-clerk for a room to change in, and afterwards walked away with her little carpet bag.

It took only moments to change into split riding skirt, white blouse and boots. She had no hat. In fact she rarely ever wore a hat. That blue-black wealth of hair was better anyway.

As she stepped out of the borrowed room and paused to close the door a quiet Texas voice drifted upwards from where the desk-clerk and the marshal were standing loosely at the registry counter. It was one of those quiet, matter-of-fact voices that went with practical men who had few illusions.

It said: "A man gets along, and his values change. He's no longer capable or even willing to fight for the things he believes in. I reckon that's the answer."

The clerk's voice came next, toned down and sounding uncomfortable. "Marshal, I lived here all m'life. I figure to go on livin' here. What old Merritt does don't concern me—right or wrong. Only, a feller

16

wonders sometimes . . . He's always been a tough old man; no one stepped on his toes."

"That's what I mean," said the marshal in his drawling Texas voice. "A man's values change."

She heard those two break up, heard the marshal's booted feet stride on across towards the door, and when she descended to the lobby only the clerk was there, and his face was unalterably closed to her. He smiled mechanically and he gallantly nodded, but his eyes were unreadable and lips were set in their accustomed secretive fashion.

She paused at the door running that snatch of conversation through her mind, stepped through just far enough to sight Jack Carson sitting up there, and studied Jack's oddly withdrawn expression.

There was something wrong at Thunder Pass Ranch!

Over across the way that lanky Texas marshal was leaning against the shaded front of Fletcher's store with a panatella stogie between his teeth, watching Carson and those four cowboys. When Kathy stepped out the Texan's black-eyed look included her. She knew he was watching her as she moved over towards the saddled, extra animal the cowboys had brought along. She knew that Texan was a full man, an experienced, seasoned hand along the raw frontier. That grave look he'd put upon her at the hotel had said this much. It had even said a little more, but she wouldn't consider what else it had said at all, for men's eyes had slightly widened at sight of Kathy Merritt before. She knew those looks, knew what they meant, and she remembered Miranda's rough comments about men with those expressions upon their faces.

Jack handed her the reins and smiled with his eyes down into her face. The four cowboys sat there eyeing her. She stepped up, settled lightly across leather, shortened and evened-up her reins, and turned away as the others also cleared the sidewalk for the northward trip to Thunder Pass. Just before she loped out though, she swung for a last look at that Texan over there in front of Fletcher's emporium. He was still watching her, watching them all. He was a rawboned man with a deceptive looseness to him, quick and solid with a cultivated expression that didn't quite hide the blaze of feeling that lay in the depths of his eyes nor down around his tough-set lips.

She followed the others over into a loose lope thinking that whoever he was, that Texan was the proper man to replace her old friend as local law enforcement officer. Then one of the cowboys laughed aloud as he carelessly said to the men loping along beside him, "Hey; d'you see old eagle-beak standin' over yonder by the store watchin' us like a hawk?"

The other cowboy said that he'd noticed, but this man neither smiled nor laughed. In fact, as Kathy studied this one's face she thought life had changed him away from ever laughing, had made him forget how to laugh. He was a stocky man with sandy-coloured hair badly in need of shearing and colourless tawny eyes that seemed cold, seemed always moving and weighing what they saw.

Jack Carson eased down a little to allow her to come up even with him. He looked over, smiled again with his eyes only, and fumbled at making conversation. "Well, Kathy; no more school, eh?"

She said, "What is it, Jack?"

Carson's smile died at once. He looked on ahead and jaw-muscles rippled under his leathery, bronzed skin. He said nothing.

She saw that tawny-eyed cowboy watching her now, saw his narrowed eyes fill with disapproval of her and suspicion. She concentrated on her riding, kept silent the rest of the way across the shimmering range, puzzled deeply and also troubled. She knew fear when she encountered it and although she'd never before met it on Thunder Pass range, she knew that she was being surrounded by it now. The closer they got to those fat-shouldered mountains the more she became aware of something musty and roiled in the atmosphere.

The heat was a pure blaze of washed out blue. It smothered the lowlands and clouded even the heights of Thunder Pass. It rolled back off sidehills with a punishing ferocity and it danced across mica particles in the dust to sting the eyes. For a few breathless months out of each year Oklahoma lay cowed under this dehydrating force. In days gone by Indians had congregated in the uplands where there was a humid kind of shade. They had named that gunsight-notch on ahead, and the reason had been an elemental one. For some reason beyond their knowing rain clouds formed up there, hung for days on end cooling an otherwise burning world, and invariably there was summer thunder. Thunder Pass, they had called it, and the name remained. No one had ever come up with a better name;

no one ever would, for whether the skin was red or white Oklahomans were an earthy, insular people who spent the long years of their lives in the service of the soil, they all had the same darkly stirring environment, red or white. Deep in their remembering blood was the pull of their native earth.

Thunder Pass had in the ancient beginning possessed a natural game trail down into what was now called Lincoln Valley, but which in those dim-distant days had been only a huge basin of protected land. Later, the Indians had padded through the pass cutting that trail deeper and wider. Still later there had been wagon-guns and soldier-columns to hack that trail into a road. Finally, Thunder Pass possessed a stageroad carefully shored up where it needed shoring, smoothed out where ridges had appeared, flattened and shaped and moulded into an excellent stageroad running northward up out of Lincoln Valley to the other settled places of Oklahoma's frontier world.

When Jared Merritt had originally carved out his cow-empire with Texan guns and his own iron will, that road had been nothing more than a military highway which bisected his range. It had become almost an artery of survival for Jared and his besieged rangeriders when unpredictable swarms of troubled redskins had struck blindly at everything the white men stood for; it had brought relief to his attacked ranch headquarters more than once. Now it was an accepted thing, like a tried, true friend, with which the people of Thunder Pass Ranch lived on equal terms. It was both their lifeline to the outer world and their source of news. But as

Kathy rode along it now towards the turn-off where an ancient, smelly old juniper tree grew, with the Merritt brand seared deeply into its shaggy bark, she wondered what else that old road had brought, for those wolfish riders cantering along behind her were, she knew, strangers to Lincoln Valley and to the Thunder Mountain country.

They left the trace at the old juniper, slowed a little before passing downward towards a broad, secret valley in the blurry foothills, and finally Carson slowed to a walk. Ahead lay the well-cared-for old log buildings, the spidery network of working-corrals, the little iron-fenced burial plot upon yonder sidehill beneath huge pines, the mighty barns and lesser buildings, including a bunkhouse, which had all through Kathy Merritt's school-years been vividly and wistfully imprinted in her heart and mind.

Farther back where the hillsides rose up towards Thunder Pass and the east-west curve of far-away rims, there was a good kind of shadowy, inviting shadiness. There were never-failing creeks and springs back in there where, as a troubled girl she'd sought her solitude and had dreamed her little-girl dreams. She knew those mountains as only the Indians before her had known them. They were friend, companion, confidant; they were her private domain.

Carson brought her back to the present by saying, "Your paw's at the house, Kathy. I'll send back for your things when the wagon rolls for town. He'll be mighty proud to see you." Jack swung to show her his carefully blanked-over face. "Miranda's been cookin' fire-cakes an' lamb since sunup. She's been countin' the days."

"How is she, Jack?"

He inclined his head. "She never changes. Those Choctaws are like the Cherokees and the Osages. They live forever, never show anything, never say too much."

"Say too much?"

He loosened his reins and leaned a little. The horse under him jumped ahead and lit down in a little choppy lope which covered the last hot mile. The four cowboys seemed to take everything Carson did as a cue; they also swerved around Kathy and loped on ahead down into the big, dusty ranch yard.

She came on slower. There were a host of memories reaching out to her now from the yonder forest, from the thrusting overhung peaks high up, from that shaded little iron-railed cemetery plot where her two brothers and her mother endlessly slept, from the mighty log barn, even from the working-corrals where she'd first tasted the hot dust of summer in her mouth after being bucked off her first unbroke colt.

It was all here, all the crowding-up yesterdays, all the half forgotten kindly rough men who had been here and who had ridden on never to return. All the frustrations, fits of uncontrollable tears which she hadn't even understood herself but which had seemed to increase after her twelfth birthday, and which had just as inexplicably departed after her eighteenth birthday. Even the dim memory of her two stalwart brothers returning in slab-boxes to go into their slots up there on the sidehill, and the not-so-dimly remembered passing of her mother. It

22

was all here in this soft-shadowed valley, sometimes vivid, sometimes dim, but none of it forgotten.

She passed down into the big yard over by the house and only half saw those four men lounging over at the barn watching her. Jack Carson was nowhere in sight. There was one more stranger, a thick-shouldered massive man smoking a cigarette over on the bunkhouse porch. She couldn't make him out too well, but she mildly wondered at him sitting over there bold as brass in mid-day when the rangehands usually were out working the ranges.

CHAPTER THREE

JARED was waiting in the parlour for her to come through the front door and when she did he neither moved nor spoke. She crossed the room with its musty old Indian blankets, shields, medicine bundles and proud lances, the impedimenta of another era, saw through a hot blur the same old massive leather chairs and marble-topped tables. And finally, she saw the lines running deeply down her father's leathery, lean old face. He was as she'd expected, entirely white now; all the grey was gone from his hair.

"Welcome home," he said softly and raised his arms.

She received his hug, brushed his rough cheek with her lips and was entirely silent. A powerful wistfulness gripped her, keeping her silent. Then the mood passed and she stepped back.

"You look well," she said, feeling around for the right words and not quite finding them because of tiredness which lay in his eyes and which she'd never seen there before.

He smiled. "A man changes a little every day, honey, only when he passes fifty the changes occur faster. Well; where are your things?"

"Jack didn't bring the buggy so I left them at the hotel and rode back with him. He'll have the wagon pick them up in town later."

He kept on smiling. He was an elderly man with nearly all the best of him gone down the years, but his gaze was still the same, steel-grey, direct and full of feeling. Something in that gaze reminded her of the lanky Texas marshal back in Thunder City.

She said, "Father . . ." and got no further. A rolling dark shadow padded soundlessly into the room from the pantry. Round, unreadable black eyes showed a soft mistiness. She ran on over to Miranda the Choctaw squaw and got a hug that left her nearly breathless.

Miranda said quietly, "Good. Big day this one. Good." Then she released Kathy, stepped back and showed concern lying tightly across her dark, moon-shaped face. "You come to kitchen by and by. We talk." Miranda touched Kathy's arm with a surprising gentleness; she did not seem to be a gentle person at all. She was one inch over five feet tall, weighed nearly as much as old Jared weighed, and for all her lightness, her grace of movement, Miranda had muscles a man might envy and there was a hardness in her, put there by an ageless heritage, which made her sometimes as unrelenting and merciless as a cougar. Once, in a rare, confiding moment, Kathy's father had told her how he'd acquired

Miranda the black Choctaw. He'd simply traded the headman of her clan seven horses. The headman had told Jared it was not a good trade for the cowman because Miranda, the widow of a stalwart warrior, hated with a depthless black passion; the reason he would get rid of her was because every time his broncos returned from a raid with prisoners, Miranda selected the toughest, most vicious of the enemy warriors, and killed him. Sometimes she did this as the man slept by simply slashing his throat. Sometimes she shot them. But the Choctaws, a relatively mild people, were afraid of the dark devil that lived in the embittered and childless widow.

Kathy had only seen that side of Miranda once. She'd been sixteen then and they'd been gathering blueberries in the forest beside a creek. Out of nowhere a frothing, moth-eaten old mad wolf had run at Kathy, who was closest. Miranda whipped around, screamed to divert the rabid animal, then from somewhere under her shapeless old sack of a dress she attacked with a knife Kathy hadn't even known Miranda carried. She had literally slashed that wolf to bits. Even after he was dead she stabbed and slashed. It had left Kathy badly shaken— not the rabid wolf, but the pure ferocity she'd seen on Miranda's face. But afterwards, neither she nor Miranda had ever spoken of that.

"She's been cookin' specialities for you all day," her father said. "I went out to get some breakfast and she said, 'Five, six hours then things change around here'." Jared chuckled. "No smile, no 'good morning', just that five-six hours remark about you getting home."

"Dad," Kathy said, "Jack's changed. And those four men—since when does Jack need an escort to ride into Thunder City?"

Old Jared's chuckle died, his smile atrophied, his lips sagged at their outer corners but his gaze didn't waver; at least that much of him hadn't changed. He said, "We can talk later, honey. You go rest and maybe visit a little with Miranda. Loaf today. We'll talk at supper tonight."

Her father put forth a hand to nearly touch her, then let it fall back, turned on his heel, strode across where his old hat hung on a rack of buck-antlers near the door, dropped the hat atop his head and walked on out of the house.

She turned and saw Jack Carson meet her father out in the shimmering yard. They spoke quietly, briefly back and forth before turning and hiking on over to the bunkhouse. She saw that cigarette-smoking burly man rise up over there and stand aside as Jared and Carson moved on inside out of sight. Then the thick-shouldered man paused to glance over at the house, flip away his smoke, turn and go on in after them. The bunkhouse door closed with a strong finality.

Kathy slowly turned and slowly walked out through the pantry into the kitchen. Miranda was at the stove, sweat making her face shiny. She glanced over her shoulder, motioned Kathy to a chair at the huge oilcloth-covered table and brought forth a pan of fire-cakes she'd evidently been keeping hot just for this moment. As she set this delicacy before the beautiful girl and went back for a glass of milk at the wall-to-ceiling insulated cooler, she said, "You finish school?"

Kathy said, "All through now, Miranda," and considered the fire-cakes. As a child she'd loved them but now there was no hunger in her at all. Still, she broke one pastry and nibbled on it.

Miranda set the milk down, pulled out a chair and lowered her considerable bulk. Indian-like, she struck directly at the thing nearest her heart, which was Kathy. "You keep away from men?"

Kathy smiled over into that solicitous, intently watching dark face, into those black eyes with their cultivated blankness. "Men don't interest me right now," she said. "Except the men of Thunder Pass Ranch. Miranda . . . ?"

"These ones the worst," grunted Miranda, and gave her head a fierce wag. "One, two good ones. Sometimes one, two good ones like here—mostly no-good ones like the others. Like Forsythe." Miranda didn't pronounce that name right. She said 'forked-sight'.

"Who is Forsythe, Miranda, and where are all the old riders?"

"All gone now. Jack here, your father here, all others sent away."

"Fired?"

"Fired. Forsythe fire them all three weeks ago. Send them all away. Have his own men." Miranda, who had once been a Sioux captive, now said with great feeling. "*Dina sica.*" No good. "All Forsythe men *dina sica.*"

Miranda sipped the milk, put the glass aside, leaned upon the table and nodded her head. "Tell me," she said softly. "I felt it down in Thunder City."

Miranda gloomily nodded; she, like all her people, was a firm believer in omens and premonitions; they were the signs people should live by. "You feel my trouble." Miranda put a hand to the valley between her breasts then pushed that palm straight outwards towards Kathy. "You knew down in Thunder City because my heart sent this message to you. There is bad trouble at Thunder Pass Ranch. Forsythe came here five weeks ago with one man—he of the yellow eyes. The others came the next week."

"What did they want; why are they still here?"

Miranda shrugged and shook her head. "I don't know. I don't have to know the black heart of my enemy, I only have to be sure of his black heart. First, all the men were paid off and sent away. Then they went everywhere with your father and Jack Carson. They were like shadows. Even out to the herds or down to Thunder City. They went everywhere. At first they would go in pairs, one pair with your father, one pair with Jack Carson. But now they only let your father or Carson leave the ranch at a time. When one is gone the other must stay. One is always a prisoner. Now—*you* are a prisoner too. You'll see. You go to ride out—they will follow you or ride with you. I got to gather berries—one is always where he can spy on me. No good, Kathy. All of this, no good. All of this is bad trouble. I sent you this message from my heart so you would be warned."

"But my father—"

"No," broke in Miranda, drawing her thin-lipped mouth down. "When he goes to bed I take his gun. It is empty. He has no bullets in his gun. You see now; you understand?"

"Prisoners on our own ranch, Miranda; but why? What do these men want; who are they; how did they ever manage to do this to my father—to Jack?"

Miranda had no answer so she sat there stolidly gazing across the table from her unblinking black eyes showing bitterness and hatred, and a certain patient craftiness. Finally she said very softly, "Now you are back, good; we can help."

Kathy waited. She had learned at Miranda's knee a lot of Choctaw ways. Silence, for instance, had as many shadings, as many nuances and colourings as grand oratory.

"You smile, I kill." Miranda's eyes shone. "One at time. Forked-Sight first. He will want your smile he is a strong man. You smile, I kill."

Kathy felt a little breathless. She was a frontier girl, death in its many forms was no total stranger to her, but this kind of death left her loose in her chair and short of breath.

"I'll have supper with my father tonight. I need more answers, Miranda. We'll wait," she said.

Evidently Miranda had expected this for she inclined her dark head. Then she said, "There is another man."

"A sixth one?"

Miranda made a little gesture with her broad hands, palms upwards, indicating uncertainty. "Maybe yes, maybe no. This one rides a big blue horse. He is a tall man who looks like a hawk. His hat is black."

Kathy instantly remembered the Texas marshal down in

Thunder City. She frowned. "He wears a badge?"

Miranda made that little fluttery gesture of uncertainty again. "I saw him now three times in the trees sitting his horse like a stone, watching. He never lets the others see him. I see him. I think he knows I see him. But the ones who watch me don't see him. I think he is a Sioux."

Kathy smiled in spite of herself. All her life whenever Miranda described men who struck fear into her she at once said they were Sioux Indians. During Miranda's brief period as a Dakota captive, she had come to mightily respect and fear Sioux men. Sometimes, when she said this about a man, she sounded almost awesome, as though Sioux men were not really men at all but were some very special breed of human beings. She would never knowingly say anything complimentary about any man, but when she said a man was a Sioux she very clearly showed respect, even admiration, although wild horses couldn't have dragged a voluntary compliment about men out of her.

"He is the new marshal down at Thunder City," said Kathy. "I saw him today."

"*Ozuye we tawatas*," rumbled Miranda gravely. "A man of war. A Sioux, that one. The others, *dina sica,* but *that* one—very bad medicine."

"You've only seen him three times from a distance, Miranda."

"*Ai;* but I know. I have lived a lot of yesterdays. I know that one."

"He was watching the ranch?"

"Yes. Still and silent like a spirit. His gun has a white

30

stock. His blue horse is very tall. He is a Sioux."

Out in the sunblasted yard a wagon rolled through gritty dust making an abrasive sound. Kathy went to a window to look out. Two of those men who had gone down to Thunder City with Jack Carson were upon the seat.

Beside Kathy stocky Miranda said, "They go for supplies. I gave Forked-Sight the list this morning. Flour, sugar, bacon, beans. A big list." Miranda paused to closely study the booted, spurred riders on the wagon. "Those two—one laughs, one never laughs."

Kathy recognised the cowboys. The tawny-eyed suspicious man sat up there with the lines in his fingers while the other man was that same bold, reckless-looking younger one who had called the Texas marshal 'eagle-beak'. She turned away from the window, went back by the table and stood thoughtfully quiet over there. Finally she said, "I think I'll go for a ride," and walked out of the kitchen back into the parlour where she hesitated a moment, then switched directions and went on through to her own room. There, scarcely noticing how Miranda had freshened the bed, the curtains, she rummaged a dresser drawer for the little pearl-handled .41 her father had given her for Christmas four years ago. It wasn't there.

Her silvered spurs were there, nothing else seemed to be missing. She sat down to put on the spurs with a leaden feeling behind her belt.

She passed back into the parlour and went to the place behind the door where her father had kept a carbine and a loaded shotgun leaning ever since she could

31

remember. Those guns too were missing.

She walked out onto the porch, saw a loafing cowboy down by the barn, stepped away from the house and kept a secret watch on that man. He saw her half way across the yard, dumped his cigarette, stepped upon it and straightened up to his full lean height. He watched her with obvious interest, obvious admiration. When she veered towards the barn he made a slow smile and drawlingly said, "You figure to go saddlebackin' ma'am?"

She nodded, coming to a halt out where the sunlight was bitterly hot.

The cowboy's smile became alert. "I'll fetch a horse for you," he said, turning into the barn.

She thought to tell him which horse, her chestnut mare, but she didn't because her tongue was like wood against the roof of her mouth. *He was going with her! Miranda hadn't exaggerated; she was now a prisoner too!*

That fierce heat drove her over into the barn's doorless wide opening where she could see the cowboy rigging out two geldings. He was still faintly smiling. She twisted to look back towards that closed bunkhouse door. There was no one in sight anywhere; it frightened her a little to see all this hushed emptiness where always before in this same yard there had been noise and movement and activity. It was forbidding, all that endless quiet.

Over by the side of the house near the geranium bed a squatty shadow slightly moved. Miranda was over there watching. Kathy felt immeasurably relieved by that although Miranda was just as helpless as Kathy was.

The cowboy came forth leading two horses. With his lingering grin and his careful eyes turned towards her he said, "Figured I'd best go along with you, ma'am. You bein' a lady an' all it just wouldn't be gentlemanly to let you go ridin' around alone."

"I was born and raised on Thunder Pass Ranch," she told him, stung to mild annoyance by his patronising attitude. "I know this country better than you do."

He passed across the reins and kept right on watching her from that grinning face. "Don't doubt it, ma'am. Don't doubt it a-tall." That was all he said as he swung up and grinned down at her; no argument, no rough-snarled orders, just those mild words and that fixed smile which said very plainly he was going along whether she liked it or not.

She stepped up, reined off northwesterly and hooked her horse hard. He jumped out and lit down running. The cowboy sprang out behind her but now he wasn't smiling. She didn't slacken off until, up near the first tier of trees, pine-sap-fragrance reached her. Then she slowed to a walk without once looking around at her shadow.

CHAPTER FOUR

ATHY'S ride was short and unpleasant. Whenever she paused those crafty eyes with their grin were upon her. The man never made an overt move. In fact he rarely even spoke, but his presence eventually made her cut short the ride and head on back.

That evening with a coolness marching down from the high peaks, with two lamps upon the supper table and with impassive Miranda padding back and forth between kitchen and dining room, she recounted her adventure to old Jared as he ate across the table from her.

Old Jared lifted his eyes without entirely raising his head. He said drawlingly, "But you knew before that, honey. You knew the second after you sat down with Miranda." His faded eyes showed their little ironic twinkle; the same little twinkle they'd shown dozens of other times across the years when he knew his daughter and Miranda had been together, discussing things that didn't directly concern them. "Women are like that; they can come to share confidences within minutes. Now with men, it sometimes takes—"

"Dad."

He let it trail off into a long, heavy and awkward silence. He ate a moment then put down his fork. "It won't be for much longer, Kathy. Then they'll head out. Maybe another week, no more than two weeks at the most."

"You have Mister Forsythe's word for that?" she bitterly asked.

Jared leaned back, his expression showing something she had never before seen in her father's face; a secretive closeness; a hardening of his spirit against his daughter.

"How did they ever come here; what made them select Thunder Pass Ranch?"

He continued to silently regard her. His habitually dead-level gaze as unwavering as ever, but blanked-over now.

"Dad; what *is* it? When I asked Jack on the way home this morning he rode away from me. Who are these men—how could they ever do this to you and Jack—and the others?"

Her father, for all his troubles and his weighty years, was deceivingly smart about humankind, especially about his only child. "Don't fret," he said softly to her now. "There's been trouble on Thunder Pass Ranch before and it's always gone away. Forsythe is a—"

"Is a what," drawled a rumbling voice from the yonder parlour, and Forsythe himself stepped through into the dining room. He was a burly-built man with a pair of cold and restless pale eyes and even when he was smiling, as now, there was no warmth at all in his face.

"Thought I'd come get acquainted with the little lady, Jared. Didn't mean to interrupt an interestin' conversation."

Forsythe moved along until he was beside old Jared and across from Kathy. His stare was bold and thoughtful as he looked. "Mighty pretty," he murmured through knife-edged lips. "Mighty pretty girl you got, Jared, an' I can tell just from the flash of her eyes she's also plumb smart. She'll be a dutiful daughter; whatever you tell her she'll do, and that's what we like around here."

Jared said mildly, Kathy thought too mildly, "Honey; this is Buck Forsythe. Forsythe, this is my daughter Kathy."

"Right proud to make your acquaintance," Forsythe said, and rolled his head sideways as Miranda entered the room, saw him, changed pace slightly then came ahead dropping her eyes.

Forsythe pulled out a chair, dropped down and hooked both elbows upon the tabletop. He had his hat on and was armed and spurred. He stared straight over at Kathy. "One of my pardners said you didn't have much of a ride today, ma'am. Maybe tomorrow you an' I can ride out ahead of the heat. It could be real pleasant."

Miranda was taking their plates. Kathy could feel her bristle, could feel the charged electricity in the room. She said in that cultivated sweet way she'd learned at Mrs. Heppelwhite's school, "I'm sorry but tomorrow I have other plans," and stood up.

Forsythe lifted only his eyes. He gently inclined his head. "Sure you have, ma'am, but there'll be other days."

This was both a veiled threat and a promise and Kathy bent to pick up several plates and help Miranda at clearing the table. As she walked out of the dining room towards the kitchen she heard Forsythe say to her father:

"Jared; what was that you were fixin' to say when I walked in?"

Jared's answer was lost behind the swung-to pantry door but as Miranda came along and put down her plates those wet black eyes looked deadly. Kathy was shocked by their fierce shininess.

Miranda said, "A man's way never change, it doesn't matter the colour of his skin. That one means trouble for you. I think we should kill him tonight—then the others."

Kathy went across to the window and gazed out. There was a sprinkling of high stars overhead and half a yellow old moon. At the bunkhouse orange-yellow lamplight streamed through the solitary small front window to show a lanky man lounging upon the bunkhouse porch smoking; there was a Winchester saddle-gun lying loosely across this man's knees. Kathy turned back.

"Miranda; do they patrol at night?"

"Always patrol, day and night. Always watch and see and be where you don't expect them. Two weeks ago I crept to the corral. One pushed his gun into my face and cocked it. No good that way, Kathy. No good sneaking out in the darkness."

Kathy moved over to the kitchen table and sank down there. Miranda padded out of the room and shortly returned with more supper plates which she put aside and looked sideways over at Kathy.

"You think?" she asked.

"Yes, Miranda. I was thinking of something I heard a man say today—that when a man gets older his values change."

"Explain."

Kathy glanced up. "My father; ever since I can remember he has been a fair man but a tough one. Now— he just sat there when this Buck Forsythe walked into the house wearing his hat and his spurs."

"*Ai;* and his guns. Always with his black gun. *Dina sica.*"

"What's happened to my father, Miranda?"

Kathy got no reply; she hadn't expected one, in fact her thoughts were moving away from that question even as she asked it.

A little later, when the two of them were washing dishes, Jared came into the kitchen, looked at them both and crossed over to lean beside his daughter. "You deserve more of an explanation than I started to give you out there, honey," he said, his voice jerky and hoarse-sounding. "They are part of the wild bunch."

Kathy's hands became still. "*The* wild bunch, Dad? Those outlaws from Nebraska who feed off the Texas trail-drives?"

"The same, honey."

She turned from the waist to look at him. He was examining his fingernails.

"Are they waiting for a drive to pass by, Dad; is that why they're loafing around here keeping us all captives on our own ground?"

"No, honey; if that was it I'd challenge 'em even if only Jack and I had to try it alone. No; they've already hit a herd." Jared dropped his hands and looked at Kathy. "I don't know any more than that though; Forsythe told me they'd hit a herd, sold it to some Texas outlaws, and came here for another purpose."

"What purpose, Dad; to kill us and take over Thunder Pass Ranch?"

"No, of course not, honey. Nothing as desperate as that. They have information about a bullion shipment coming south through Lincoln Valley bound for Texas. They're waiting to catch the coach over on the Pass road. They don't aim to do anything more than take the bullion—no killings."

"Forsythe said that?"

"Yes." Jared caught the first hint of a scornful expression of his daughter's face and shook his head at her with a darkening scowl. "There won't be any killings, I'm satisfied on that score for a good reason. You see, one of the guards with that coach is Forsythe's man."

Kathy stood gazing at her father. She was filled with wonder, with a slow, paralysing sense of disillusionment. "How can you be a part of this, Dad? How can you stand by while these—"

"Kathy, just let me tell you one thing—then you explain to me how I could have acted otherwise, Forsythe and one of his men were in Thunder City for one full day and night before they came up here. They hid four charges of dynamite with concealed fuses. They put a fifth charge under the jailhouse. That fifth charge is the one Forsythe told me about. The other four only he and that yellow-eyed rider named Frank Canton know about. Kathy; if I send out word by whatever means what Forsythe and his bunch is here to do, and the law or the army comes here—one of those men will try to get down to town and blow the place up.

"Those four buried charges, Forsythe said, each contain six sticks of powder. Kathy honey, have you any idea what twenty-four sticks of dynamite exploded in the heart of Thunder City would do?"

Miranda, who had been intently listening to all this, brought up a chair and put her hand upon Kathy's shoulder; the girl's face was white to the hairline. She looked ill as she sat down under the pressure of Miranda's broad hand.

Her father went on speaking. "Now honey, you tell me what else I can do, and I'll do it. Taking my guns and ammunition, keeping Jack and me prisoners here and firing all the old hands, even making you a prisoner too, I can live with for as long as it takes to see this thing through. But if, because I'm an old man, I've overlooked something and you can tell me what it is, I'll do it with my bare hands."

There was a long interval of depthless silence when Jared ceased speaking and somewhere over across the yard a man's exultant shout resounded. Kathy, even Miranda, started. Jared didn't bat an eye.

"Every night they have a poker game. Someone just won a big pot."

The stillness re-settled in the kitchen and ran on to its very limits. Kathy got up and walked to the window. In faint starshine that armed guard over there on the bunkhouse porch with his tipped-back chair and his ready Winchester seemed not to have moved.

"But why us?" She whispered without turning. "Dad . . . ?"

He said, "Call that part of it Fate, honey, but that's not

very important." He looked ahead at old Miranda. "Any coffee in that pot?" he asked, indicating the stove with his chin. Miranda didn't reply, she wiped both hands, got a thick crockery cup and went over to fill it. She brought the cup back, handed it over and said, "There is a poison made from blue lupin."

Jared looked down his nose over the cup's rim and shook his head. "They're smart men, Miranda. You never see all of them together. All it would accomplish if we killed one or two of them would get *us* killed." He lowered the cup, swished its black-oily contents and frowned. He was waiting for Kathy but it was a long wait, and after a time he said musingly, "When I was a younger man I knew men like this Buck Forsythe, but in those days they fought with guns and sometimes they died hard, but they never did anything like *this;* never planned the systematic destruction of maybe a hundred men and women and kids and destroyed a whole town."

Kathy turned finally. "I'm sorry, Dad, for what I thought. I've never had any reason to doubt you. I don't know why I doubted you now."

"What else could you think?" he said with a bitter shrug.

"It's so—so—unreal. So fantastic."

"Give Forsythe his due, honey, he's a smart man."

"A devil, Dad. He's *dina sica.*"

"*Mala hombre* the Mexicans say, honey, but it amounts to the same thing. The only good I can see coming from any of it is that Buck Forsythe has planned so well that I don't think there'll be any bloodshed. Not if we go on co-operating and not if that guard with the coach does his part well."

"Oh he'll do his part well," said Kathy with bitterness dripping from her words. "Without knowing him or ever even seeing him, I can tell you he'll do his part well."

Jared put aside the cup and turned. "Well . . . ?" he said.

She folded both hands across her stomach. "Your way is the only way, but afterwards—"

Jared broke in with a low growl. His face changed completely. In a second all the resignation was entirely gone. "Never you mind the afterwards, Katherine," he said stiffly. "That's *my* end of things."

When her father called her Katherine instead of Kathy, even as a small child, she knew what it meant: There would be no compromising, no arguing, not even any pleading.

"No, you go on to bed, honey, you've had a hard day. And Kathy, one last thing: Don't. Whatever ideas pop into your head—don't. There are too many lives at stake. You understand?"

"I understand, Dad. I won't do anything. Just one more question: You said they might be here a week, maybe two weeks. Don't they actually know when that coach will be along?"

"Forsythe says they don't. He told me the stage line isn't letting anyone know when they mean to send the coach southward. That seems to be the only hitch. But when the right stage comes through Thunder Pass that armed guard will signal with a mirror."

"I think I see now, Dad. Thunder Pass Ranch, being most isolated yet nearest to the road and far enough from town to give the outlaws a long lead, was chosen for exactly those reasons. Dad; you were correct; Buck Forsythe *is* a smart man. I'll see you at breakfast, good night. Good night, Miranda."

As she neared the yonder door her father said softly, "You'll get used to it, honey. After a few days it'll even seem good to be able to save Thunder City and all those people. Anyway, don't worry too much. And Kathy—it's almighty good to have you home for good."

She smiled back at him, at the dark, solid figure of Miranda at his side, then pushed on into the farther rooms. Around her the house was silent and the faint starshine came in past uncovered windows. She had the feeling of being in the only really safe place on the ranch, this night; that outside lurked indescribable evil.

CHAPTER FIVE

UNLIGHT seared the world catching upon anything shiny to hurl cruel reflections upwards. Heat dropped down layer upon layer of it as the morning advanced until it became a gelatin weight that sluggishly moved as Kathy and her horse pushed through it.

Buck Forsythe rode just behind her sweating profusely and holding his eyes nearly closed even under the tugged-forward broad brim of his hat. Forsythe was suffering; he didn't like heat at any time. He'd originally come from the upper Powder River country of Montana, and while the summers up there were hot enough, they had never been anything at all like the furnace-breath of Southwest summers. Still, a man could tolerate discomfort, at least a little of it, if the eventual reward was sufficient.

That was what Forsythe thought as he poked along behind Kathy, but that was not all he thought. A man much alone has also his secret, gentler thoughts, and now Forsythe's expression showed that these private notions were also uppermost in his mind, because Kathy Merritt was a beautiful woman and lonely men, outlaws or not, had their dreams, their hungers, and their longings.

Kathy halted at the creekside, dismounted to drink and to afterwards lightly bathe her wrists and face. It alleviated the heat slightly as it always did, then, as Forsythe came forward to do the same she watched him with a great curiosity.

He was a cold man, she could see that, and a carefully calculating one with his broad, low forehead and his unflinching eyes. She wondered about his background, his life, the things which had formed him into what he now was. Then he turned, saw her watching, eased down upon creekside grass tipped back his hat and said, "Evenings are better for this sort of thing, unless of course a person has some special reason." He looked hard at her. "You don't have some special reason do you?"

She shook her head.

"Your paw talk to you?"

She nodded a second time.

Forsythe's cold expression loosened a little. "Then you know how things stand, and that's just fine. Maybe it won't be much longer." He plucked a stalk of cured grass, popped it between his strong teeth and briefly ruminated. "No one gets hurt when they do like they're told. If they don't . . ." He shrugged, spat out the grass stalk and gazed at her with his speculative, cold eyes, which she thought were slightly overcast with worry or perhaps impatience.

She said, "Why Thunder Pass Ranch? Why didn't you just make a camp up near the top-cut, Mister Forsythe?"

He relaxed. It was pleasant there with the soft chuckle of the little creek, with the fir-tree-shadows lying thickly all around. "Good enough reasons. You can't make cookin' fires for three, four weeks up atop a hill without travellers and cowboys wonderin'. At your ranch we're just riders; no one pays us much mind."

"You're wrong."

"Am I?"

"The local people will wonder. No matter how isolated a ranch is, there are always others familiar with its work-habits, with its people and its schedules. When strangers suddenly appear to have taken over, folks will wonder."

He showed her his wintry smile. "What folks wonder about doesn't worry me. It's when they get too nosy and come ridin' around to snoop that I worry. So far we've had no snoopers." He kept his level, cold look upon her. Abruptly he said, "You're beautiful. You've heard that before, though. A man always has time to notice a woman like you."

She sprang up, caught up her reins and stepped up over leather. She gazed down at him. "Every day you remain on the ranch lessens your chances. You surely must realise that."

He got up slowly, almost lazily, brushed off dead grass and stepped to his horse, as he toed in to mount up he said, "You know, it's an odd thing, but I never lived on a ranch this long before." As he settled across his saddle and evened the reins he said, "I can see where it'd get to be a comfortable kind of monotonous existence."

She led him on across the little creek and up into the gloomy trees where cathedral light came filtered downward through stiff-bristling limbs. The day droned on. She had no destination in mind; it was just pleasant to be atop her chestnut mare again passing all the places she'd known since childhood. She didn't even have any fear of Forsythe behind her, riding along with perspiration lying heavily across the flat of his cheeks and faintly darkening his butternut shirt. He wasn't enjoying this ride, she knew that, but he was a man of endless patience; he wouldn't ever complain. But when he'd had enough of something he would make his prompt decision and issue his sharp order for it to end. So far he hadn't issued any such order so she led him up and across and downward through the hills to a little grassy meadow where a bell-cow's clear clarion-call showed them both a small herd of perhaps two hundred critters grazing down there, their tails swishing almost in unison at summertime's everlasting horn-flies.

She halted atop a little brushy lip of land and watched

the cattle for a while. Forsythe sat beside her also watching. Finally he said, scorn blurring his words, "Each cow makes you fifty dollars a year and to get it you've got to be nursemaid, veterinarian, wheelwright, blacksmith, book-keeper and weather-prophet. You spend all your life worryin' about dumb brutes an' you make a living that sometimes you don't have the time to enjoy. Cowmen got to be dumb-brutes themselves not to expect anything more of life than that."

She said sweetly, "But it's a rewarding life, Mister Forsythe—and a long one."

He didn't miss that innuendo. "When a man passes fifty he gets miseries; aches when it rains, pains when it's hot, worries all the rest of the time. Me, I'll take mine in big doses of cold cash, live hard and go out quick."

"Do you hate life or does life hate you?"

He thought on this, couldn't come up with a decent answer and jerked his head. "All right. You've had your damned ride. Now head on back. And ma'am, don't go ridin' tomorrow. I've had enough of this and you're not foolin' anyone."

She didn't ask what he meant, she simply reined around and started back. As the humid silence rolled back for them to pass through she speculated about Forsythe. There was no room in his life for so many of the things which made life not only good, but bearable. He'd said she was handsome, and yet even when he'd said that his gaze wasn't soft nor agreeable; he'd made a statement of fact, that was all. How long did it take a man to squeeze out all the frailties which made him human and retain only the things which made him efficient?

Just before they left the trees she twisted to say, "There are many people in this world who pass entirely through it without ever really seeing very much. Did you know that?"

"I know this," he said, sweeping the onward shimmering plain with half-closed restless eyes. "There are lots of things in life that can distract a man, turn him weak an' undecided an' futile, an' most of those things are the result of abidin' by man-made laws."

He suddenly yanked back on the reins to stand his horse perfectly still. Over on the stageroad there was a little thin whipped-up banner of dust moving southward. Kathy saw this and also saw Forsythe's dark profile with its quick interest. "A pair of riders," she said. "Maybe three of them, no more. But it's not a stagecoach, Mister Forsythe."

"You got good eyesight, girl."

"No; it's just that I've spent most of my life out here. I've seen all the different kinds of summertime dust-banners hundreds of times. After a while you get to know exactly what causes each kind."

He grunted and dropped back to considering the onward, heat-cowed land with its layers of shimmering brightness and its endless hush. He was becoming impatient she knew, was beginning to feel the ennui which to men of his breed was the next worst thing to death, the total inactivity, the monotonous days-on-end waiting which rubbed nerves raw and put tempers on edge.

His shoulders were broad and powerful against the background forest-shadows. He was a big, confident man with violent, dark emotions behind all that calculated outward coldness. He could kill without a second thought, and she thought, when his turn came, he would die the same way. But for as long as he lived Buck Forsythe would never cease to be a menace to everything which law and order stood for. He wasn't just an outcast, he was also an inherent misfit.

"What you starin' at?" he growled.

"You," answered Kathy boldly. "I was wondering how a man became as you are."

"How am I?"

"In one word? I'd say treacherous."

"I can slap you out of that saddle, girl."

She inclined her head. She had up until several hours ago been very afraid of this man. Now, for some reason she wasn't fearful of him at all. It wasn't entirely because she was a woman or because she had no gun; it wasn't even because she knew a secret about him now—that although he might look at handsome women with the ancient hungers of men, he actually had no use at all for them. It was something else: Buck Forsythe's exterior cold poise only imperfectly concealed a crawling, frustrated sense of increasing impatience at all this endless waiting and watching and keeping up his pretences and his vigilant guard.

He was a violent man but he was also an active one; the worst imaginable thing which could happen to an active man was this enforced inactivity. She said, "I hope someday you find what you want out of life, but I don't think you ever will," and eased her horse forward out into the pitiless sunblast. He swore, she heard that, then he also pushed ahead out of the last fringe of tree-shade.

It took them nearly an hour to get back down to Thunder Pass Ranch's massive log buildings, every inch of it under the unnerving force of that dehydrating heat. Just before they entered the yard Buck Forsythe said, "Remember what I said—no more of this pleasure-ridin' in the heat of the day."

There were two of Forsythe's men lounging in front of the barn, they kept their careful eyes upon her until she dismounted, looped her reins and walked away. She heard one of those men growl as he stepped out to take her horse into the barn and that pleased her. There was an ancient inherent wisdom in women, Miranda, old and ugly as she was, still had it; Miranda had known how Kathy's presence on the ranch would change things; she'd realised it long before Kathy had. Now Kathy knew this too, but she also knew something which just might prove to be an even better weapon. There was a simmering impatience in those outlaws. It could be very dangerous to play on that and yet it was tempting.

When she entered the house Miranda met her in the parlour, her black-eyed look close and also reserved. Kathy asked where her father was. Miranda said he'd gone out for an hour before, then she asked if Kathy had seen that Sioux of a white man with his ivory-stocked .45 while she and Forsythe had been riding.

She hadn't seen the Texas marshal. In fact she hadn't even thought of him and said so. Miranda kept watching her. "You will," she pronounced. "He will be out there watching."

They went together into the kitchen. Kathy was ravenous. While she ate she also ran through her mind all the little pieces of a human puzzle she'd encountered this day, worked them up into the composite which was Buck Forsythe, filed them away for future reference, and told Miranda where they'd gone and how dry the forest was. She also told her of Forsythe's swift, hopeful look when that distant cloud of dust had appeared. Miranda stoically listened and offered no comment until, clearing away Kathy's dishes, she cocked her head, stepped to the window and looked out. Then she said, wonderingly, "That's yellow-eyes. They sent him out to keep watch this morning. Why does he come back now?"

Kathy walked over to also gaze out into the yard. The mounted man out there was leaning down to quietly talk with Forsythe. There was something in both their faces that was speculative. Miranda eventually dourly grunted and stepped on over to her sink to clean the dishes but Kathy kept watching. Something, some kind of a crisis, had appeared, she felt certain of that; she knew Forsythe now well enough to know that when he spoke in swift short bursts as he was now doing to that mounted man, something untoward had either happened or was shortly going to happen.

She started to step away but at the same moment Forsythe jerked his head, tawny-eyes headed past on over towards the barn and Buck Forsythe stood out there a thoughtful moment staring hard at the house. Then he started sauntering towards the porch.

Kathy slipped out into the parlour, waited a minute for the expected knock, and when it came she went quickly forward, all her female curiosity aroused. Whatever it was that now troubled Forsythe was about to be revealed to her. She opened the door.

Without any preamble the burly outlaw chieftain said, "You listen good to what I got to say: There are two men ridin' in from the stageroad. One looks like a preacher or something and the other one is that hawk-faced marshal from Thunder City. I got no idea what they want, but you talk to 'em and you remember—I've got your paw. He just walked in down at the barn. If those two so much as look suspicious, your paw's a dead man. Think you can remember that?"

Forsythe's gaze was brittle; there was no admiration in it now and no steady but restless patience. This was, she thought, the way he looked when he cocked a gun in some bank clerk's middle or when he hit a trail-herd camp, or when he had stage drivers and guards under his gun. Deadly, resolute and ready.

"I can remember."

"Then tell 'em your paw's out on the range and get rid of them." Forsythe's lips drew far back. "You're a pretty smart female, Kathy. See to it that you use your smartness for the right things now. It's not just your paw's neck that's involved, you better remember that too."

Forsythe stepped back, turned and hiked purposefully on over to the bunkhouse. She watched him all the way. He called up those two lounging men down there, spoke briefly with them then passed on into the bunkhouse, closed the door, and seconds later she caught the dull sheen of a carbine-barrel at the window's gloomy edge.

CHAPTER SIX

HEN the Texas marshal and his riding companion came down into the yard Kathy was watching from the parlour window. Although she didn't know it Miranda was also watching from her kitchen window, and Miranda was galvanised into action at sight of that bronzed man wearing the black hat. She swept out into the parlour with her usually reserved glance showing quick, hard excitement.

"*Dakota!*" she exclaimed breathlessly. "The Sioux is here!"

Kathy looked around and looked back. Over at the bunkhouse that blued barrel was no longer visible. At the shoeing shed one of Forsythe's men, stripped to the waist, was bending over to fit a shoe to his horse; he was facing towards the house as he did this, his head tilted a trifle too high. In one of the pole-corrals a man was patiently stretching a lariat, snapping it to get the kinks out. He too was facing the yard as he seemed to be concentrating upon his chore. It was all very innocent looking to Kathy. It was also very lethal looking. She had no idea whether or not Forsythe's other men had her father prisoner in the barn but she had no intention of taking any chances either. At least not openly.

Miranda shuffled forward to stare out through overhang shade where those visitors had dismounted and were now securing their animals at the rail. She made a little trilling sound in her throat which Kathy understood—it was the Choctaw signal to beware.

"I don't see him this close before, Kathy. He is a tall man. His face is strong."

"Do we have anything cold to offer them?" Kathy asked, also intently watching that lanky man.

Without a word Miranda left the parlour on her soundless moccasined feet.

Just for a second as he started on up towards the porch the Texan slowly turned and ran a light look out and around. The man with him wasn't, as Forsythe had speculated, a preacher, he was old Doctor Ford the only physician and surgeon for three hundred miles in any direction. Ford had brought Kathy into the world; he had come here in the early days, a Northerner, and he had stubbornly remained even when the war had come and Oklahoma's strong Secesh sympathies had made life difficult for him. He was an old man now. In spite of the heat and burning brightness his face was pale. He wasted no time getting in under the porch roof.

Kathy opened the door to him; she held it open for the Texan to also come inside. Doctor Ford smiled at her and muttered something about it being devilishly hot and how lovely she looked, all in the same breath.

When the marshal paused in the doorway to put a solemn downward gaze upon her she felt lifted up by his stare, felt as though his examination of her was clinical, as though he was comparing her to someone else, perhaps to a strong memory that lived with him. He had strong cheekbones and thin lips that came definitely together. He struck her for some reason as a man who didn't say a whole lot, and also as a man who, despite his almost lazy movements, could move with the speed of light when he wished to. Right now he didn't wish to.

Doctor Ford made the rough introductions and afterwards turned as Miranda entered the room bearing a tray. "Ah," said Ford sounding immeasurably relieved, "what have we here, Miranda," and lifted one of the glasses with a little gallant bow from the waist toward Katherine. "To you, my dear, who have grown into a breathtakingly beautiful woman. To you and to everything you wish for in this life."

Miranda passed over to the tall Texan, her black eyes as steady and wide as they could be. The marshal put aside his hat, returned Miranda's look, lifted a glass, sipped, and said in guttural, sliding Choctaw "Good."

Miranda moved away without showing anything in her face or saying anything. Kathy took the last glass and asked the men to be seated. She saw the sidelong way Miranda was intently watching the younger man.

"Well," said Doctor Ford from the cool comfort of a huge leather chair, "it was worth it after all. I told the marshal before we started it would be a wasted trip; that no one at Thunder Pass Ranch ever got sick."

"Sick?" said Kathy, easing down across from the quiet Texan.

Ford made a grimace. "For forty years when people don't show up regularly in town, the busybodies get to gossiping. You know how it goes, Kathy. By the way; where's Jared?"

"Out on the range," lied Kathy smoothly, and a little red colour climbed into her flushed cheeks. "Did you expect to find him ill, Doctor?"

"No, of course not, but to quiet the naggers I agreed to ride out with Marshal Belmont. You see, he gets this same nagging, Kathy."

She turned politely towards Marshal Belmont. He had one leg crossed over the other and both hands crossed atop the higher knee. He was studying her from an expressionless face. His hands were wide and heavy at the knuckles. There was a quiet deliberateness about him that said he took his time about everything. He was at least six feet two inches tall and looked to weigh close to two hundred pounds, which was not heavy for so tall a man, but that weight was well-distributed. His shoulders were wide, his flanks lean, his arms packed with a solid power from much hard work. It was his calm regard of her though that now put her on guard. This would be a very difficult man to play-act in front of. He had that invariable advantage all quiet men had; he let others act out their thoughts, their schemes, while he sat back assessing, probing, listening, making his careful judgments and his correct decisions. She could imagine him facing down gunfighters and rough rangeriders without ever speaking. If he could laugh or smile she saw no sign of it now. In a way all this put her on the defensive. It troubled her.

Then he spoke and his voice was effortlessly slow and deep, it was, she thought, a soothing voice. She also thought he knew that and would use his deep drawl to throw others off their guard.

"Like Doctor Ford says, ma'am, when folks start rumours it's either his job or mine to spike them."

"Rumours, Marshal?" she said in that soft-velvet tone she'd learned to use at Mrs. Heppelwhite's school.

"Just talk, ma'am."

Ford drained his glass and put it aside. The intake of liquid had inspired his sweat glands to working furiously. He mopped his pale face with a limp handkerchief and stuffed the thing back into a coat pocket. "Jack hasn't been around much, Kathy. He used to ride in now and then for a session of poker, but we haven't seen him for a month now."

Doctor Ford's jovial face was reflective, his smiling eyes were suddenly not smiling at all. Kathy could sense the feelings of these two. Neither of them was going to put anything into words, and in fact they were going to act as naturally like themselves as they could, but there was that feeling she got, an instinctive thing, which told her plainly enough that both Doctor Ford and Marshal Belmont had been garrulously complaining about the futility of their ride to Thunder Pass Ranch as an actual cover-up for their real curiosity.

Miranda came back to re-fill the glasses. She was her usual silent, impassive self until Hyde Belmont said to her in Choctaw: "Trouble has many masks but its smell is always the same."

She stiffened from filling the last glass, which was Belmont's. She gazed a moment into his lifted, sun-darkened slightly hawkish face. In the same tongue she said gutturally, "A wise man rides where the fragrance is sweet. A fool rides in where he smells trouble."

Belmont slowly inclined his head. He and Miranda exchanged a long look then the squaw turned and left the room. Belmont's eyes, behind the half droop of lids, keenly followed her exit.

Kathy forced a little annoyed smile, saying, "Marshal; not many people speak Miranda's language any more."

He swung his gaze over to her. "Everyone has secrets, ma'am," he softly said, and kept right on watching her.

She felt her interest in this man heighten considerably. The room was temporarily quiet. Doctor Ford was on his second glass of cold tea, sweat running in rivulets down across his face. The yonder yard was as still as death, its clearing brightly glittering under the wilting overhead sunlight. Marshal Belmont sat over there with his mouth ruggedly set, showing solemnity and interest. His wide shoulders were solidly outlined against the chair. They were strong. In the running-on quiet Kathy was aware of his very careful attention.

He was an unusual man and because of this, plus a natural interest in him because he was a man, his presence preyed constantly upon her mind. She tried to assess him as she'd earlier assessed Buck Forsythe, but Hyde Belmont was not so elemental in his drives. He was more complicated, more difficult to understand. She did understand, however, that behind his seeming quiet indifference lay a dagger-sharp mind, a power of observation uncommon in men. His calm eyes back of their drooping lids were sharp. His attention to detail was careful and thoughtful. He would be a hard man to deceive. Finally, there was a shade of tough irony in his eyes that plainly said he controlled his judgments of others as well as of himself and his personal actions.

But there was more, much more, which she could only sense, and without the time really; because she had to work hard at fooling this man, she couldn't probe any deeper. Not that she thought her probing would expose any more. A person could only reveal the inner workings of vanity and intelligence to be shared. Hyde Belmont, she conceded, was more than her equal.

Doctor Ford settled in his chair with a little rustling sound; also, he settled back with a degree of finality which gave Kathy her first clue that these two were not just here to pass the time of day. They had some preconceived plan. Some very definite reason for what they were doing. She decided to seek out this reason.

"Doctor; tell me the news of town. I haven't had a chance to ride down."

Ford mopped his face again and smiled limply. The cool tea, the humidity of the cool interior of the room, were making him drowsy. "Not a whole lot ever happens, Kathy," he said and cleared his throat as a thought occurred to him. "Well; Marshal Clampett got killed last winter. It was a sad day, believe me. It happened when he was making one of his routine rounds of town after nightfall. He came upon some men out the back of Fletcher's store trying to break in. He hailed them and they opened up on him. He never even got his gun out."

Ford waggled his head dolorously back and forth. He and Clampett had been friends of long standing. He raised his eyes as though to shake clear of something bitter. "Hyde was riding through, the City Council hired him the next day—and we buried poor Clampett."

"What of the men who shot him?"

Ford rolled his head. "Ask him," he said, meaning the quiet tall Texan. "He went after them."

Kathy looked over. Marshal Belmont's gaze was still upon her. Instead of directly answering her unasked question he said, "I had an interesting talk with an older man named Gallagher about four weeks ago, ma'am. Whip Gallagher. Did you know him?"

Kathy knew Whip Gallagher. He'd been a Thunder Ranch cowboy since she'd been in pigtails. "I knew him, Marshal. He used to work here."

"So he said, ma'am," drawled the law officer, his unswerving eyes boring into her. "Whip was saddened at bein' let go. He had a lot of fine memories stored up. We sat in a saloon most of one afternoon just talking."

"Did you?" said Kathy, beginning to worry about this man. "Well; all that happened while I was away so I couldn't be much of an authority on it, Marshal."

"On what, ma'am?" asked the Texan mildly.

Kathy flushed, seeing what she'd done. He hadn't asked her why Gallagher and the other riders had been fired, but he'd led her into making an admission that something had happened out at Thunder Pass Ranch.

"On nothing," she said sharply, and stood up looking stiffly over at Belmont. "Is there anything else I can do for you?"

Hyde Belmont didn't answer and he didn't stand up for almost a full minute afterwards, but he eventually did, and he carefully shaped the crown of his black hat, which was already shaped, studied the results and dropped the hat upon the back of his head. Their eyes met again, this time she looked upwards and he looked downwards.

"About those men who shot Marshal Clampett," she murmured. "Or would it be a useless question to ask, Marshal?"

"Not useless, ma'am. Futile maybe but not useless." He glanced over at Doctor Ford. "It's turning cool out, Doc. Maybe we'd ought to head on back. There's nothing here anyway."

Kathy watched the medical practitioner struggle up out of his chair with a series of little grunts. On the spur of the moment she stepped to her father's little writing stand, took up a pen and hastily scribbled across a scrap of yellow paper. As she straightened around she saw Hyde Belmont soberly watching her. She smiled.

"Just something I remembered to add to the list of provisions when we send the wagon into town again, Marshal. If I don't make a note of those things I forget them."

"Sure," he drawled, and stepped on over to the door, opened it, held it for Ford to pass through, then faintly nodded. "It's been a pleasure, ma'am," he said smoothly.

She crushed the little paper in the palm of her hand, walked on out across the porch with them, down to the hitchrack and as they mounted up she put forth a hand to scratch the right ear of Marshal Belmont's tall blue horse. When her fingers encountered the leather keeper below the headstall buckle she inserted that scrap of yellow paper, pushed it down hard and dropped her hand as the lawman lifted his reins and touched his hatbrim. In the same unsmiling way he said, "We're much obliged for the hospitality, ma'am. Maybe we'll pass through again real soon."

Doctor Ford straightened his frock coat, muttered a curse towards the evilly glittering sun, threw Kathy a wave and pulled his horse around. She waved back, stepped clear, watched them ride on over the yard and afterwards stepped up into the shade of the porch. Her heart was furiously beating. Like everything people do recklessly, on the spur of the moment, she was suddenly afterwards filled with all kinds of recriminations, all manner of self-reproach.

The slumped-forward older man and his companion were out where the heat waves distorted them when she heard the hard crunch of boots from around the side of the house, the soft music of spurs, and turned.

Buck Forsythe was there, his cold eyes showing what she took to be grim approval. He walked on up, stopped beside her and also looked far out. Without lowering his eyes Forsythe said, "You did famously, Kathy. I was out back listening. You didn't over-act or under-act." Forsythe swung his head and lowered it. He was considering her differently now. She could sense something close to approval.

She said, turning away towards the house, "Send my father back now," and walked on inside leaving him standing out there gazing after her. It had been a deliberate slight. He said something coarse under his breath and continued to stare at the house, then stepped down and went hiking on over towards the barn.

Miranda was waiting and as Kathy turned to watch Forsythe Miranda said, "It would have been better to hand it to him. Now, it might fall off his bridle."

CHAPTER SEVEN

DON'T know what made me do it, Miranda. Just on the spur of the moment I simply had to do *something*—anything at all. Don't tell my father."

Miranda grunted and jutted her chin. Coming on across the yard was Jared, his hat tugged low shielding his eyes, his step stiff and awkward as though he were angry. Kathy moved to open the door.

Across the yard two men sauntered forth from the barn to lean in the afternoon shade over there. Another man crossed towards them from the shoeing shed and Jack Carson came from around back where the working-corrals were, in company with Forsythe's tawny-eyed roughrider. The lot of them converged where Forsythe was, near the barn's big opening. Kathy saw Forsythe speaking and wondered what he was saying.

Her father passed into the house, reached over to push the door closed and swung his head from Kathy to Miranda and back again. "Doc Ford and that new lawman," he said. "What brought them out here?"

"People in town are wondering why none of us have been in," explained Kathy, then more slowly she said, "Dad; what do you know about the new marshal?"

Jared hung up his hat, went to a chair and dropped

down. He was red in the face. "You got something cold to drink?" He asked Miranda, and when she left the room he put back his head to rest it and to also lift his line of vision to reach Kathy across the room.

"Not much, honey. He's a Texan. I've only seen him a couple of times. You see, Forsythe showed up on the ranch about the time he took over old Clampett's job. Haven't any of us been to town much since then. Why do you ask?"

"I have a strange feeling about him, Dad."

Jared gazed a moment over at Kathy then raised his eyebrows slightly. "Oh?" he said. "What kind of a strange feeling?"

Kathy crossed closer to her father and eased down upon a couch. "As though he knows a lot more than he lets on, for one thing. As though he can tell the moment someone lies to him."

"Well," responded old Jared dryly as Miranda brought him a glass of cool tea, "I hope he isn't that smart, daughter, because if he is—and if you didn't do as good a job of deceiving him as Forsythe seems to think you did, we could be in trouble."

Kathy's conscience bothered her. She kept thinking of that spur-of-the-moment note she'd put in Hyde Belmont's bridle keeper. She knew he'd find that note and read it. It frightened her to think of what he might do. He certainly hadn't impressed her as a rash or reckless man and yet one never knew about people.

She got up to pace across as far as the door and back again. Jared sipped tea and watched her. Out in the yard a horseman went jogging across in the same direction

Belmont and Ford had taken. Through the window both Kathy and her father saw this man ride on out.

Jared said in the same dry voice, "Forsythe doesn't miss a bet. He's sent that one out to make sure Doc or the Texan don't slip back."

Kathy's heart stood still for a second and over by the pantry door Miranda turned and put a slow, knowing gaze over at her, then glided on through towards the kitchen.

"I think I'll go riding," she said suddenly.

Jared's gaze clouded up. "You just came back before Doc and that Texan rode in."

"It's cooler now though, and anyway, Dad, I'm restless."

"Kathy?"

"Yes."

"Remember what I told you: Whatever you're thinking—don't. You remember?"

She nodded over at him, went to the door and passed out to the porch. Down at the barn Buck Forsythe and Jack Carson were standing in sulphurous shade talking. They saw her up there on the porch and their conversation dwindled. She stepped forth and headed directly towards them, but at the last moment she didn't mention going riding to Forsythe, she simply smiled up at Jack, completely ignored the outlaw chieftain and moved on into the cool, shadowy depths of the high-vaulted old barn.

Her chestnut mare was tied in a stall. There were several other animals tied inside too, and the obvious reason for this made her wry. No matter how certain outlaws were of anything, they also proved that they weren't sure at all by keeping get-away horses close at hand.

She strolled ahead gazing in at each horse. They were fine animals, the kind that if men paid money for them they would cost a small fortune. From behind her a deep voice with a little tart drag to it said, "Figurin' on settin' 'em loose and puttin' us all afoot, Kathy?"

She turned, met Forsythe's cold smiling glance, faced forward and sauntered along studying each animal as she came to it. "That wouldn't do any good. You'd only get more horses."

"Sure, but not like these." Forsythe stepped to a particular tie-stall and leaned there considering a powerfully muscled-up very handsome big bay horse. "He's mine and there's not a horse in Oklahoma, or Texas either for that matter, that can stay within rifle-shot of him. He's a thoroughbred."

She paused, turned back and looked up at Forsythe's face. His tone had quietly softened as he'd spoken of his beautiful big bay horse and now she saw something in his face that genuinely surprised her—affection.

She moved back to also gaze at the bay, and she said, "Did you steal him?"

He looked around and down. "Let me tell you a secret, Kathy: Any time you have real need for animals as good as these, never steal 'em—buy 'em."

"Oh?"

"This bay of mine, for instance; every time I ride into a strange town folks notice him right off. He's one in a half million and he sticks out. If he was a stolen horse folks would find out in no time at all. You can't own animals like this and not have folks always asking questions about them. So you pay good hard cash-money for them, get a plumb legal bill-of-sale, and there's no trouble—not until you do to that town what you went there to do—then, when the posses bust out after you, there you are, a mile ahead on the fastest horse in Oklahoma—laughing fit to kill." Forsythe was near to smiling. He swung back to admiring his big bay horse. "I gave a thousand dollars for that animal, Kathy; more money than I knew there was in the whole wide world until I was nearly twenty years old. And these other horses—also the best. My boys don't ride anything but the best. You see why I don't think much of cow-ranch horses now?"

She didn't answer. From the corner of her eye she caught sight of a man moving down towards them from up front. It was Jack Carson, his face full of strain and worry. Forsythe swung.

"I told you to go on over and stay in the bunkhouse," he snarled. Kathy saw instantly that towards men Buck Forsythe was totally cruel.

Jack kept right on coming ahead. "I know what you told me, Forsythe, but Kathy here happens to be like a little sister to me."

Forsythe waited until the rangeboss halted then said, "I told you a dozen times, Carson: Nothing will happen to her if she doesn't try anything cute. Now do like I told you—go over and stay out of sight in the bunkhouse."

Jack hung there trading looks with the outlaw chieftain. Kathy knew her father's rangeboss as well as anyone did.

Jack had no fear in him. He was an intensely loyal man with a degree of warmth which was rare in rough frontiersmen.

"Come along," she said, beginning to feel something violent forming up in the space between those two men. "I'll go sit with you, Jack." She took Carson's arm and dragged him around. They were almost to the barn's doorless opening when a rider showed up dead ahead. It was the tawny-eyed man whom Forsythe had called Frank Canton. Kathy's legs suddenly became leaden and the roof of her mouth became very dry. Canton had been out spying on Doctor Ford and Marshal Belmont. If anything had happened, if Belmont had happened to find that note before he got back to town, Canton would have something to say. She squeezed Jack's hand bringing him to a halt just outside the barn and to the right where Forsythe didn't see them halt but where the oncoming man had a very good view of them, particularly of Kathy with her white blouse.

But Canton came across to the barn steadily eyeing them, swung down and stepped ahead as Forsythe came out to meet him. Forsythe also saw those two over there idly standing. He scowled and his mouth went flat because Carson hadn't obeyed him, but when the tawny-eyed man said, "Nothin', Buck. Just pokin' along on their way back to town with the old one lookin' like he's goin' to melt in that buryin' coat he's wearin'."

Forsythe nodded. "Put up your horse," he said to Canton and turned. But Kathy was walking on over to the bunkhouse again, Jack Carson pacing along at her side.

Afternoon was coming into its period of pre-dusk quiet. Somewhere far out men were driving cattle along. The dust rose straight up and hung in the breathless air. Kathy stopped to watch and Carson said with drawled indifference, "Forsythe sent three of them out to cut out a fat steer and fetch it in to butcher. Miranda told him they were getting low on meat."

Kathy looked upwards, asking a question that had intermittently been bothering her. "Jack; why don't they eat in the kitchen like our hands used to do?"

His eyes darkened with ironic amusement. "Forsythe doesn't trust Miranda. I heard him say she'd poison the lot of them the first chance she got."

They went up onto the little bunkhouse porch into stifling shade, Kathy murmuring, "He's right of course."

Inside, men's belongings lay carelessly scattered but one thing Kathy noticed at once. There wasn't a gun of any kind in sight. She took a battered chair and sat down upon it, nodded at the rangeboss's holstered .45 and lifted her eyebrows. Also in pantomime, Jack Carson lifted out his gun, opened the gate so she could see the cylinder, and spun it. Like her father's gun, Carson's weapon was also empty.

As he leathered his useless weapon Carson dryly said, "Give the devil his due. Forsythe's no fool."

"He's the biggest kind of a fool, Jack." Then, after a quiet look out into the empty yard she lowered her voice and told him what she'd done.

Carson leaned over there on the door-jamb blankly considering her for a full minute without speaking. He turned and shot a look up and down the yonder yard, turned back and quietly asked: "What did you write in the note?"

"I didn't have time to say much," replied Kathy. "I said there were five hidden charges of dynamite in Thunder City and that one of them was somewhere around the jailhouse. If he finds that one, Jack, he'll know it's the truth."

"Kathy; you did a foolish thing. Your paw and I've been taking Forsythe's guff for a month just so's no one in town would have to die. Now, what you've done is maybe spoil all that and endanger a hell of a lot of folks."

"No Jack; Marshal Belmont can be trusted."

"Can he? Kathy; for all any of us know he could be one of the wild bunch. Forsythe and these four men with him aren't all of them, and they've got friends all over Oklahoma."

"He seems so—"

"So did Forsythe when he first rode in here, girl," said Carson roughly, and turned to cast another alert look out and around to be certain no one was close by. "We don't know anything at all about this Belmont except that he just happened to show up in Thunder City the same day Clampett got killed."

Kathy said faintly, avoiding the rangeboss's eyes, "You make it sound terrible, Jack. All I was trying to do was let him know so he could try and find those bombs and get them out of Thunder City."

Carson lapsed into a long silence, his solemn face creased with fresh worry. Eventually he said, "You're paw'll have to know, Kathy."

She sprang up, breathless. "No, Jack. Please . . . He

asked me not to do anything. Please; don't say anything just yet. Anyway, that yellow-eyed one who just came back said the marshal and Doctor Ford were riding back as though nothing had happened. Maybe the piece of paper dropped to the ground."

Carson showed strong disapproval but he ultimately agreed to keep her secret for a few days; he even said hopefully that perhaps Hyde Belmont wouldn't find the paper. Then he unmercifully upbraided her for that one rash act.

When she left the bunkhouse finally, along towards suppertime, she felt as though she had betrayed her father and their rangeboss as well. Carson had made her feel that way.

CHAPTER EIGHT

DAWN came to the southwest with a pink freshness rarely found anywhere else. It had its own regional scents and sights. It was in many ways the most beautiful time of day, particularly in summertime, for then there was that short time before the heat came, when all the world was clean and clear and soft-scented with its composite odours of cured dry grass, greasewood, sage blossoms, pine-sap and other ingredients.

Kathy left the house before the sun was quite up. It lay beyond the far curving of a distant east, its golden light firming up over the horizon, its promise of violent heat not yet fulfilled. She went to the barn, started saddling her chestnut mare, and a thick shadow fell across her before that little job was half finished. She lifted her head not knowing which one it would be, and recognised that empty-smiling man who had ridden forth with her that first day home. He was smiling now as he'd smiled then; it was the same kind of a smile wolves use when they have a fawn cornered in the mountains.

"'Mornin', ma'am," this outlaw said, and grounded his Winchester in barn-dust to lean across it watching her work. "Sure lonely aroun' here at night when a feller's walkin' sentry-go. You know; I figured when the war done got over with, I'd never have to walk no more sentry-goes, an' that just shows how wrong a feller can be, don't it?"

Kathy finished saddling, took down the bridle and stepped to the mare's head. Now the outlaw straightened up, put forth a detaining hand and, still vacantly smiling into her face, shook his head.

"No'm; I reckon you'd best just wait a spell. Buck'll be along directly. He always comes down to look in on his horse ahead of breakfast. We'd better just sort of set a spell until he gets here. Then, if he says it's all right for you to go ridin' in the cool of the mornin', why hell, I'll even bridle her for you."

Kathy said: "Your kindness overwhelms me," and stepped clear of that detaining hand. The outlaw's smile broadened, deepened, became genuine enough.

"Spitfire, ain't you, ma'am? Well, us Missouri boys got all the blindfolds, the hobbles—and the quirts—to take the rough edges off heifers like you. But hell, I don't really blame you a whole lot; I reckon in your boots I'd be sort of edgy too. As a matter of fact I'm fixin' to get a little that way myself, just from this everlastin' waitin' around. It's enough to drive a man to dippin' snuff, for a pure fact."

Buck Forsythe stepped through the yonder doorway, halted and gazed ahead. "She trying to ride out?" he asked roughly of the Missourian, but that grinning man shook his head.

"Naw; just wants to ride a little while it's cool, I reckon."

Forsythe didn't look pleased. In fact he seemed to be in a vile mood this early in the day. He glared at Kathy, walked on into the barn, glanced around at the other animals, saw that they'd been fed, evidently by the Missourian, and finally dropped his eyes back to Kathy again.

She said, giving him look for look, "You said not to ride out in the heat of the day so I thought I'd do it now ahead of the sun."

Just for a second Forsythe's black look darkened, then he glanced at the Missourian. "Go with her," he growled, turned and hiked back out of the barn.

The grinning outlaw put aside his Winchester, brought forth a solid sorrel and rigged it out. All the time he was doing this he was quietly smiling as though something was inwardly amusing him. Then he finished bridling both animals and handed Kathy the reins to her mare, picked up his carbine, dumped it into the saddleboot and swung up.

"Let's go," he said.

She mounted and rode on out into the yard before

saying, "Have you been on guard all night?"

"No ma'am. Just since midnight."

"But have you had breakfast?"

The Missourian chuckled at that. "A feller in my trade learns right early to always have a little somethin' in a pocket, ma'am. Yeah; I've eaten."

They rode northward. The land was brightening along towards daylight. Visibility was excellent. Kathy could make out all the details of the onward sidehills and their ranks of erect, dark-barked trees.

She rode steadily but without any hurry because she had no destination, really, only a desire to get away, to be clear of all those closed faces back there, those intent eyes and long silences.

She had left even before her father was stirring. Miranda alone knew where she'd gone, but Miranda the Choctaw had said nothing one way or the other. Even in Miranda the crisis was approaching.

It was something one felt. Something that seemed to increase as the heat would shortly also increase after the sun jumped up out there in the brilliant east. It was the inevitable result of so much waiting, so much monotony.

She rode along deeply breathing, seeing her forest and her Thunder Mountains in all the cool, pink freshness of an unspoiled pre-dawn morning. Behind her the Missourian jogged along seeing none of this, seeing only the onward shadows for whatever they might hold which could imperil him. Once, she swung to look back. The outlaw returned her look and glanced away again. Like Buck Forsythe, this man also inhabited a separate world from the great majority of people. And yet he smiled easily. Not always genuinely but easily, which meant that life hadn't really overwhelmed him at all, hadn't turned him bitter and ruthless and cold, as it had Forsythe. She thought of the two men, Forsythe would be the most predictable. The Missourian was not an outlaw because something had driven him to it. He was an outlaw because he wanted to be one, so, despite his easy manners, his talkativeness, his sometimes-vacant, sometimes-genuine smile, he was the worst of the two. He had no reason at all for being what he was, except his inbred cruelty.

But she had no fear of her companion. Survival mattered to this man exactly as it also mattered most to Forsythe and the others of his wild bunch. They might harm a girl in some brief, thoroughly relaxed, thoroughly safe moment; they undoubtedly would and it wouldn't bother their consciences at all, but they would never be pulled off guard by a lovely woman when their survival was in danger, and it would be in danger in their eyes during any illegal undertaking they were involved in, such as this business Buck Forsythe had brought them to now.

She lifted her face to the fresh, warm morning air and flung back her wealth of jet-black hair. The chestnut mare stepped along willingly, daintily, and where they splashed down through a clear-water creek their enormous shadows sent trout-minnows scurrying in wild panic.

It was cooler in the forest. The fragrance was stronger and unchanging. Rough-barked old trees stood eternally massive, their shadows added to other shadows making a pattern of light-slivers and a dark carpeting of gloom underfoot.

They passed around the curve of a mighty hill and the Missourian said in his nasal voice, "Must be good huntin' up in here, ma'am." He said that so matter-of-factly that just for a second she was casual towards him as she would have been towards a paid cowboy.

"There is every kind of big game in the Thunders, even bear and lion."

"And Injuns," said the Missourian, swinging his head left and right. "Now that's good huntin'. Them other animals, well, when a feller's hungry they're fine. But me, I like the sport of huntin' somethin' that hunts right back at you."

She looked over at him as he urged his horse on up beside her in the levelling-off country under that mighty hill. He was a lean, course-featured man in his middle years with little puckered-up eyes that missed nothing, seemingly, and one of those long, loose mouths that could be generous or brutal, laughing or snarling. He rode his horse with an easy grace. There was a thoroughly deceptive mildness about him. At least she thought it was deceptive, but when she thought of another deliberate, lanky man, she thought that this outlaw couldn't really fool other men; he could deceive only women.

They came out above a big broad valley with a tumbling white-water creek chewing up its mouldering banks on its southward coursing, and halted up there.

"Good feed," observed the outlaw. "Good place to

maybe hold a herd."

"Until you found the right buyer?" she asked ironically.

He missed her exact meaning but he caught its implication because that was precisely how he was also thinking. "Yep; hold maybe a couple thousand head in here until the hubbub died down." He made his easy, oily smile. "I got to remember this place, damned if I don't."

"It won't do you any good to remember it," she told him. "This is Thunder Pass Ranch land. All of this up in here. After you accomplish what you've come into this country to do, you'd better never return."

He leaned back, looped his reins, and fished in a shirt pocket for the makings. He kicked loose one booted foot and bent to making his smoke. With the hint of that vacant smile across his dark face the Missourian said, "Ma'am; you got a lot to learn about life. Now you take this here hidden valley for instance." He paused to lick the cigarette paper, fold it over, pop the thing between his lips and scratch a match along the underside of his left leg, light up and exhale. "We could come back here within six months—a year at the most—and you wouldn't never even know we was here with a herd. Folks got awful short memories. Awful short." He inhaled, exhaled, turned and smiled. "No one'd hear cattle bawlin' from this here place and no one'd come a-lookin' that we wouldn't know about it before they got within a mile of us. That's how Buck works at hittin' trail-herds, ma'am. You tie up with a good man like Buck Forsythe, and you got damned few worries."

"Someday you're going to be surprised," she murmured, and drew back from the ledge to twist back and forth on a downward game trail. He followed along behind letting his horse do all the work, smiling, saying nothing, smoking and thoughtfully gazing down into that big green valley below. That's how he was riding along when the low limb struck him, or at least he afterwards vigorously swore it was a low limb, but the blow across his head was so solid that he was lifted from the saddle, flung over backwards in the air making a complete turn in the air, and landed face-down to all intents and purposes stone-dead.

Kathy had no idea anything had happened until the riderless horse jumped ahead bumping her chestnut mare. She turned, saw him lying back there, instinctively reached out to catch his horse, and drew her chestnut mare to an immediate halt.

A rawboned shadow moved out away from a big tree and steadily, silently regarded her. It was the Texas lawman. He had a pine limb in his right fist.

She was too startled to do anything but sit up there big-eyed and breathless for a full minute.

Marshal Belmont dropped his club, stepped over and toed the Missourian over onto his back, regarded him for a moment then knelt and rifled his pockets. He didn't take anything off the unconscious man but he read a letter and rummaged through the man's worn old dog-eared wallet before he replaced these things and stood up to dust his knee, shoot her another solemn look and wait.

He wasn't going to speak first, she saw that, so she said, "I died a hundred times last night after I put that note in your headstall. They sent out a man to spy on you and Doctor Ford."

"Sure," he said matter-of-factly. "They'd do that, ma'am." He moved over to offer her his hand in dismounting. She swung down without any aid and faced around towards him. They were very close, so close the dark cut of his head and shoulders blocked out all the backgrounding forest to her.

"You liked to wore me to frazzle ridin' up and down these cussed game trails, ma'am. I had to leave my horse back yonder and do all this on foot." His eyes gravely twinkled in a way that somehow reminded her of her father. "And this walking business is something I just never cared much for." He looked around at the raggedly breathing Missourian and looked back. "I found the note a couple of miles out but I figured they might be watching, so I waited in town until after midnight then came back up here to watch the ranch. When I saw you come out this morning and later on ride up this way with your escort, I just trailed along waiting for the right time."

He stepped back a little, ran a long glance up and down her, pushed back his hat and waited. She stepped over to gaze at the outlaw. He was shallowly breathing and there was a sullen, puffy welt across his forehead. He would sleep for a long time. She turned back saying, "You hit him awfully hard, didn't you?"

"Why no ma'am; you can't kill his kind by knocking them over the head. Now, about that note . . ."

"You didn't believe it," she said, giving him her dead-level regard.

"Yes'm, I believed it. Right after I found that dynamite bomb under the back-end of the jailhouse buried near a crawl-hole, I believed it. What I want from you now is the location of those other bombs."

She explained that she had no idea where the other bombs were hidden and he mulled that over, coming eventually to an obvious conclusion: Forsythe had *meant* for that jailhouse-bomb to be discovered to lend credence to the fact that there were other hidden bombs in Thunder City. Then he struck out on an altogether new tangent of speculation and strolled over to stare at the unconscious Missourian.

"I'm wondering if this one would know," he said pensively.

She shook her head at him. "Forsythe is no fool, Marshal. He wouldn't tell them all just to prevent what you're thinking right now. If you could catch one of his men and make him talk . . ."

He walked back to her, his quiet gaze thoughtful. "But you said Forsythe and one other man hid those bombs in Thunder City."

"Yes. The other one is named Frank Canton. He's the yellow-eyed man who never speaks first and who never smiles. Wherever you find Forsythe, Canton isn't far off."

"You've gotten to know them pretty well these past few days," he murmured, studying her.

She blushed in spite of herself and was angry at him for making her do this. "Well enough." She cocked her head at him. "Better than I know you."

"Miss Kathy; I made up my mind yesterday to remedy

that. I even thought about it that first time I saw you—at the hotel the day you came home."

She ignored this remark and said, "Even our rangeboss, Jack Carson, isn't sure of you."

This seemed to amuse him. With a wicked little twinkle he murmured, "I don't know Jack except by sight, but I can tell you this—I haven't trusted *him*. You see, ever since I had that talk with your former rider, Gallagher, I've had my suspicions about what could be going on out at Thunder Pass Ranch. Carson's come in for his share of suspicion and so has your paw. Ma'am, I don't know any of these men a cussed bit better'n they know me, and that doesn't help any of us, does it?"

"I trust you, Marshal," said Kathy, and when she saw his gaze soften towards her she swiftly turned away and nodded over at the unconscious man. "You'd hardly have hit this one over the head after sneaking over half Thunder Mountain if you were one of them."

When she looked back the softness was gone from his gaze. He dryly said, "For a woman, Miss Kathy, you're pretty smart. Now tell me—why is Forsythe doing all this?"

She recounted all she knew of the bullion shipment, about the treacherous armed guard and also about the mirror-signal he was to make from the crest of Thunder Pass. He listened, said nothing, and went back to the Missourian as a wet groan came forth from the outlaw's lips.

"He's coming round, ma'am. You look after him. I got a heap of ground to cover." He didn't even look over at her again, he simply stepped back into the forest and faded from sight.

She stood a moment looking over where he'd been, then another bubbly groan brought her back to the immediate present. She went to the moaning outlaw, lifted his head, cradled it and used a little handkerchief to dab at the bad swelling across his forehead. When he eventually opened pain-dim eyes and saw her bending over him he struggled a little to get clear, to sit up, and almost the first move he made with either arm was to drop his right arm straight down and feel for his holstered sixgun. It was still there.

He sat a while moaning and rocking back and forth before he tried to stand. She helped him. Later, she even helped him mount his horse and led the burdened beast slowly back down out of the mountains. She was positive the Missourian had no idea what had happened to him.

Just before they came down to the sunlighted open country he asked and she told him he'd struck a perpendicular pine limb as he rode along. He accepted this without question, but right then for some hours afterwards he was in no condition to believe anything else.

She led him straight down into the shimmering ranchyard and wordlessly left him with two of his friends at the barn. The other pair were too stunned to even question her. Then she went on to the house and didn't emerge again that day.

CHAPTER NINE

ORSYTHE sent Frank Canton up to Thunder Pass the following day. Kathy saw Canton leave the ranch with a light blanket-roll aft of the cantle heading straight up into the easterly hills. She could surmise without any effort Canton's destination. She could also guess what had prompted it.

Aside from the Missourian's injured head, Forsythe and the others were becoming nearly worn-thin with impatience. The crisis she'd seen coming several days earlier was closer than ever now. The way those men acted now there very well could be bloodshed when that stage showed up despite their former good intentions. They were even beginning to snarl at each other. They had been waiting now for more than a month. That was too long for ordinary men who were not surrounded by enemies, but for Buck Forsythe and his outlaw-crew it was easily three weeks too long.

She told her father what she suspected Canton had been sent out to do—search the far country for that bullion coach. Later, when she went down to the barn and met Carson there she also said practically the same thing to him.

But with Carson the conversation took a different turn. With lingering disapproval he mentioned the Texas marshal. She told the rangeboss exactly what had happened to the Missourian the day before and Carson intently listened, his eyes upon the packed ground. Finally he looked up and she saw the first glimmerings of hope in his face.

"Then he's on the level," Carson said, meaning the Texan. "Or else he'd have ridden in here yesterday to tell Forsythe what you'd told him."

"He's on the level, Jack," she said. "He hit that outlaw hard enough to nearly kill him. If he hadn't been on the level he certainly wouldn't have done that."

They had time for no more private talk because one of the outlaws walked into the barn from out front, paused to wipe sweat off his forehead and eyed the pair of them before walking on up. "Lady," this man said, "you ain't goin' ridin' no more. Buck's been too easy on you as it is, but with one of us abed with a sore head we can't spare no more riders to go with you. Them's Buck's orders." The man gazed straight over at Kathy. "For my part I don't see why he ever let you ride out in the first place. But then I reckon Buck always did have an eye for a pretty woman." The outlaw swung to consider Jack Carson. "Rangeboss," he said, "you better head on back to the bunkhouse. We got a feller over there with a big headache. He'll need someone to fetch an' haul for him. Go on."

Carson's face darkened. He glanced at Kathy then stepped past on his way out of the barn. The outlaw followed his progress until Jack disappeared then swung back towards Kathy again, his expression cold, his eye unfriendly.

"Lady," he said, and got no further. Buck Forsythe walked into the barn, saw those two and jerked his head at his man.

"Go help with the butcherin' out back," he growled.

That other man at once walked away. Just before he did this, however, he shot Kathy a baleful look. She thought the man was resentful towards her for something she thought had to do with Buck Forsythe.

Out back somewhere men's voices came now and then where a big three-year-old steer was hanging by the heels being skinned out and gutted. Forsythe, walking towards her, cocked his head briefly to listen, then he halted saying, "You could've taken my man's gun yesterday and got away when he got knocked out by that overhead limb. I'm curious, Kathy; why didn't you?"

She half turned so that shadows shielded her face. "The idea occurred to me, but I thought he might be badly hurt, might even be dying. No matter who he is or what he's done he deserved better than to be left up there on the mountain to perhaps die alone."

Forsythe pondered this. She couldn't tell from his face whether he believed her or not. "You were smart, whatever your motives," he murmured, closely watching her face. "If you'd run off we'd still have had your paw. Maybe that occurred to you too."

She shrugged. "What difference does it make; I brought your man back, that's all that matters."

"I reckon so," responded the outlaw chieftain still closely watching her. "Like I said, you're a smart girl. If that damned old black squaw over at the house had half your sense we wouldn't be doin' our own cookin' at the bunkhouse."

She faced him squarely. "Suppose Canton finds the bullion coach; when will you leave Thunder Pass Ranch?"

This seemed to touch a nerve with him. He scowled at her. "Is that all you got to do over at the house—spy out windows?"

She didn't answer, she said, "The sooner you get that gold the sooner you leave our ranch. That's my primary concern. If Canton sees it and signals from the top of the Pass will you take your men and go?"

Forsythe's annoyed scowl lingered but his speculative eyes turned crafty. "We'll go," he assented. "But just in case your smartness is getting too far ahead with its plannin' maybe I'd ought to tell you, you and the squaw, Carson and old Jared are goin' with us. You'll get to see a genuine stage robbery you can tell your kids about someday. After we've got the gold and you folks are all afoot, we'll say good-bye to the lot of you—and good riddance as far as I'm concerned."

Forsythe stepped past, walked on down through the barn and halted in the rear doorway to glance southward where his men were sweatily butchering that big steer in thin barn-shade. He teetered there briefly looking on and saying nothing, then he turned and walked back up where Kathy stood. Her gaze never left him; Forsythe seemed to be steadily changing, to be becoming steadily more morose and edgy.

He scowled and jerked his head. "Go on up to the house," he growled, "and stay there." To this order he bitterly added a snide comment. "You can sit by the window and spy to your heart's content—you'n that treacherous-lookin' squaw of yours."

She went along a few feet ahead of him on out of the barn, into yellow sunblast where powdery dust jerked to life underfoot and was several feet past the door when she heard Forsythe enter the bunkhouse and curse. She turned. Jack Carson, she knew, was in there with the Missourian. Just for a moment there was a quick, hard stillness, then she heard Carson's cold, precise words answer back. She had known Jack Carson most of her life; when he used that very clear, very precise way of speaking he was fighting mad. What held Kathy rooted out there in the withering sunblast was the knowledge that Jack had no way of protecting himself except with his fists while Forsythe was armed. Also, Buck Forsythe, while an inch or two shorter than Carson, was easily five years younger and forty pounds heavier.

Suddenly Buck Forsythe staggered back out onto the small bunkhouse porch, turned to grab a post, missed and landed down in the bitter-lighted dusty yard on both feet. His hat was lying in the doorway up there. She hadn't seen it happen yet she knew that Carson's control had slipped; he'd lashed out and struck the outlaw chieftain.

From inside, the Missourian cried out, startled: "Hey . . . !"

Jack came through the bunkhouse door moving fast, driving straight at Forsythe out in the yard. That sharp outcry from the Missourian brought two heads thrusting around the corner of the barn where the butchering was in progress. Those men saw Carson hurtling ahead at Forsythe. Kathy glimpsed just for a second, the total surprise on those two faces, then Carson's blurring form shot past dragging her glance along with it.

But burly Buck Forsythe hadn't been hurt, he'd only been taken completely by surprise with that first blow, had been belted off balance. Now though, he was recovered, was solid-set to meet the onslaught of the lighter, taller man.

Just short of his target though, Carson slid to a quick halt. Forsythe threw a heavy punch that fell far short. Carson ducked down and jumped in, struck Forsythe in the middle and jumped back out again. Now those two men over behind the barn came running. In the bunkhouse doorway the Missourian was standing with his fisted sixgun, wetly blinking out into raw sunlight. He couldn't shoot, neither could the other two. Carson and Forsythe were mixing it, stepping this way and that but always close.

Kathy heard the front door slam hard over at the main house but didn't look around. It would be old Jared rushing across the yard, she knew that without looking.

Carson suddenly halted, his bare head lowered, his rangy shoulders rolled up, his big-knuckled hands drawn together as he sidled one way then the other way probing for an opening. Kathy, who had seen men fight before but who knew nothing of the science or the tactics of this kind of brawling, thought Jack was fearful of Forsythe's considerable power and wanted to out-jab the outlaw chieftain. She was pulling so hard for the rangeboss she almost forgot to look at Forsythe. But when the outlaw leader spoke, she saw him smiling, his cold eyes full of flame and cruelty. Her heart sank. Forsythe was too confident.

Carson stepped in to draw Forsythe forward then stepped back again. It didn't work. Forsythe kept moving, balanced up onto the balls of his feet, but he wouldn't be drawn off guard.

Carson's eyes had a red gleam now. He was completely cold, completely concentrating. This was his only chance and he knew it. To watch every move, to draw every second to his advantage. He flipped a looping jab in and out, in and out. Forsythe battered down those little strikes; he rolled his head away and swung back and forth from the waist. Forsythe, Kathy saw with dread and hatred burning in her, was vastly more experienced at this type of thing than Jack Carson was. Her father started past. She caught his arm and hung on, dragging him to a halt. Those other outlaws were grinning wolfishly now. They had their guns out but they didn't mean to use them; they were silently laughing at Kathy, at her father, at Jack Carson. They knew something those others didn't know—that Buck Forsythe's reputation included an awesome ability to fist-fight.

Carson saw an opening and rushed ahead. He caught Forsythe up along the temple and lower down, over the heart. He hammered him mercilessly with both hands driving the heavier man to turn away from those stinging strikes, but although Carson put everything he had into those blows Kathy could see with a sinking heart, they were not punishing the solider, heavier man at all. Forsythe was still grinning.

She could hear croupy breath singing in and out of Jack Carson's tortured lungs. She saw Buck Forsythe slowly turn straight into those hailing blows, still smiling. She saw Forsythe chop a vicious blow into Carson's soft parts and cross over with another blow that jarred Carson.

Forsythe went to work with a will and a deliberate purpose that seemed inexorable. He hurt Carson, bashed his mouth until claret flew, whipped Jack's head violently backwards and sank a big fist wrist-deep into the foreman's belly. He reached to catch the sagging man, caught Carson's shirt and struck him repeatedly in the face. Carson's arms hung loose and his body flopped. His head pitched forward. Forsythe ground a hard fist against jawbone. Carson's knees buckled. Forsythe still held him upright although the rangeboss was now totally beaten and unconscious. He systematically worked at beating Carson.

Kathy cried out. Old Jared jumped ahead but one of the other men met him head-on and slammed his pistol-barrel into the older man's chest. He would kill, Kathy saw that. So did her father; he stopped stock-still with his eyes and the deadly milky eyes of that gunman locked.

Kathy ran ahead and tried a trick Miranda had taught her as a child. She was desperate; very obviously Buck Forsythe meant to beat Jack Carson literally to death. She swung her left leg in between Forsythe's moving two legs to form a quick lock that tripped Forsythe. He tried to catch his balance, failed, and fell heavily with Carson beneath him. He rolled off and looked up. That other outlaw now grabbed Kathy from behind and swore heartily as she fiercely struggled.

For a moment Forsythe watched this, then turned his head, spat aside and lumbered back upright. He was breathing hard. "Let her go," he growled, stepped across unconscious, wrecked Jack Carson, turned his back upon all of them and walked stolidly across to a water-trough where he dunked his head, flung off water and gave a bitter-toned order.

"Take the three of 'em up to the main house an' throw 'em in there. Both of you stand guard so they don't come out again. I'm sick of this whole god-damned outfit."

Up in the bunkhouse doorway the Missourian was looking much better. He even grinned as those two straining outlaws picked up limp Jack Carson and dragged him indifferently along behind Kathy and her father over towards the main house.

CHAPTER TEN

CARSON didn't come around until early afternoon. His nose was cracked across the bridge, his lips were purple, swollen to twice their normal size, and leaked blood. He breathed with great difficulty. Jared said he thought some of the rangeboss's ribs were broken but Miranda, much experienced at this sort of thing, disagreed.

It was Miranda who made the poultices and washed away the sweat, blood and grime, removed Carson's ragged shirt and patiently fed him a spoonful of broth at a time. She did all this efficiently, with minimal movements, but never once showed anything in her face, no friendliness nor compassion.

Kathy and her father were in the parlour when Buck Forsythe came across to the house freshly dressed and washed, showing no signs of the battle, walked boldly in and levelled a thick finger at Jared. Forsythe looked savage. "You keep this damned girl in the house from now," he said, grinding out each word to Kathy's father. "And the next time any of you over here tries anything I'll bury you. Merritt; I'm giving you my word about this. Stay in the house and don't—"

Forsythe broke off suddenly and whipped around. Someone over by the barn had sharply called out. Kathy and her father, opposite Forsythe, able to see out the window, saw one of the outlaws running swiftly towards the house. Something was wrong.

Forsythe stepped back outside, moved off the porch and halted for that moving man to rush on up to him. The door was open. Kathy and her father heard that outlaw say breathlessly, "Buck; there's riders comin' in from the southeast," then Forsythe and his man walked swiftly away.

Kathy started for the door but her father reached out to restrain her. "Stay here," he ordered. "Those men are like blind rattlers right now. They'd as soon shoot a woman as a man. Close the door and stay inside."

Miranda appeared in the pantry doorway, her black stare shiny with hard interest. "Four men coming on horses," she reported. "I see them out back." Miranda's gaze hung on Kathy. "One is the Sioux."

It took nearly fifteen minutes for those riders to walk their horses on into the yard. By then Miranda, old Jared, and Kathy, were watching from the parlour.

Jared said, "I'll be damned. It's that Texas lawman, Doc Ford and a couple of the boys from the Kurt ranch." He began to worriedly frown. "What'll they be wanting?"

Kathy said nothing. Her heart sank. If Hyde Belmont had brought those four as some sort of posse he'd made a terrible mistake; he'd need three times that many men— and if Buck Forsythe, from his hiding place in the bunkhouse, suspected anything . . .

"Kathy," Miranda said, intently staring out into the diminishing brightness of a searing afternoon. "He isn't coming to the house. He's going to the barn. No good. Big trouble come now, I can feel it."

Marshal Belmont was indeed leading his companions over to the barn where one of Forsythe's men stood with an exaggerated look of idleness. Kathy moved over to the door, eased it open and strained to hear what was being said down there, but Marshal Belmont's soft-deep voice was too low. She caught only the ripple of sound as those two spoke back and forth briefly.

Forsythe was nowhere in sight. She knew he would be lying in ambush inside the bunkhouse again. As she eased the door closed again and briefly leaned upon it, it suddenly came to her that Forsythe wasn't only lying in ambush; he didn't want that lawman to see him. Perhaps he just preferred to remain unknown to Hyde Belmont, and then again maybe his face was sufficiently well-known for him to prefer to keep it out of sight. She thought it was the latter.

Jared said, "He's coming over here to the house."

Kathy stepped over and looked. Belmont was the only

one walking on over. He'd left his horse at the barn tie-rack along with his three companions. She was curious, more so than she'd been before, and moved back to open the door.

Marshal Belmont removed his black hat, teetered in the doorway but did not enter the house. He pushed out his big right hand saying in a slightly louder than usual voice, "Mighty nice seeing you again, ma'am."

Kathy took the hand and instantly felt a tight-folded piece of paper against her palm. Without batting an eye she shook Belmont's hand, dropped it, closed her fingers over the paper and said, "Please come in, Marshal."

He looked around the room in a ranging way, shook his head and said, this time in the same loud voice but looking on over at Jared, "No thanks, ma'am. We're on the trail of some riders who rustled about fifty head from the Kurt place. Thought they might've driven across your range and been seen." Belmont jerked a thumb over his shoulder. "But your rider down at the barn says no one's come around." Belmont nodded as he stepped back from the open door. "Reckon they must've gone on due west." He put his hat back on, touched the brim to Kathy, turned upon his heel and went back across the yard towards his horse and his waiting companions.

Kathy didn't close the door, she simply stepped around so that it hid her, unfolded the note, read it once, re-read it and moved over to the fireplace where she knelt and struck a match. Jared watched all this but neither spoke nor moved. He was charily keeping an eye upon the yonder yard where Marshal Belmont and his friends were turning to ride on westward out of the yard.

For some time after those riders had departed no one came near the main house, but shortly ahead of dusk Forsythe walked over. He walked in without knocking, pushed on through into the kitchen where Miranda was preparing supper, looked gloweringly at the squaw, who gave him back the same kind of a detesting look, then he went through the house until he found Kathy and her father in there with battered Jack Carson. He glanced indifferently at the raw effects of his fists then fastened a cold, suspicious stare upon Kathy.

"What did that damned lawman want?" he demanded.

Kathy, in the act of wringing out a fresh cool damp rag for Jack's puffy, discoloured face, looked coldly at Forsythe. "He was looking for some cow thieves who'd raided the Kurt ranch range. He wanted to know if we'd seen anyone like that passing through."

"What'd you tell him?"

"That," said Kathy, turning back to bend over Carson upon the bed, "is a stupid question. Of course we haven't seen anyone riding past. How could we, cooped up in the house like this?"

Forsythe's stare at Kathy's back hardened. "Don't give me none of your smart answers," he said sharply. "You're livin' on borrowed time as it is; the whole damned bunch of you." He stepped around where he could balefully regard Jack Carson. "And you, mister, your time done run out about two hours ago when you thought you could jump me. You're as good as dead."

Forsythe was turning to stalk back out of the room when old Jared said bleakly, "You kill anyone on this ranch in cold blood, Forsythe, you'll have to kill the rest of us too."

Half twisted in the doorway Forsythe gently inclined his head. "All right you damned old fool. I've been wonderin' exactly what I was goin' to do with you. If that's the way you want it, why hell, all I got to do is tell Canton that. He'll sock the bunch of you away and never even miss supper."

Now Kathy spoke up. Her voice was knife-edged. "You fool," she said to the outlaw chieftain. "You're not as smart as I thought. If that's what you're going to do to us, why should we bother co-operating any longer?"

"I'll tell you why," snarled Forsythe, "because you don't want to die—none of you do. So you'll go right on co-operatin'."

"You're wrong," stormed Kathy, dagger-points of pure anger turning her smoky eyes nearly black. "You've guessed us altogether incorrectly, Mister Forsythe, and I'll tell you something else, too. We can fix it so that you won't be able to rob that bullion coach."

"Like hell you can," exploded the angered outlaw. "If you could've you'd have done it long ago."

"Idiot," ranted Kathy. "We didn't try before because there's no coach yet. But we can fix it right now—within the next hour—so that you'll not only not get the coach, but you'll have to run for it."

Forsythe studied Kathy with a sneer. "How?" he demanded.

"By setting fire to this house, that's how. A big fire in this country draws every cowboy and every rancher for miles around."

Forsythe stood stock still staring at the girl. Very slowly his eyes drew out in speculative thought. Jared and Jack Carson were also staring at her. Even Miranda, who had appeared silently in the yonder hallway, drawn there by the sound of those angry voices, seemed suddenly to appreciate Kathy's suggestion.

Jared seemed troubled and hopeful at the same time. A man did not consider lightly the total destruction of his home, and yet, just as clearly, a home was no good to a dead man.

Finally Forsythe pushed out a big arm and leaned there in the doorway. He seemed to be considering what to do with Kathy. He seemed wholly absorbed by her presence to the exclusion of everyone else. His nostrils flared and he said, "I should've had Canton take care of you that first day. He was right; he said you were trouble ten ways from the middle."

Jared's lips parted as he took one long step ahead, but it was Jack Carson back on the bed partially concealed by the others who spoke first. Jack said with great difficulty and in a voice not easy to understand, "Forsythe; you touch her—so much as lay a hand on her—and so help me I'll—"

"You won't do a damned thing, cowboy," broke in Forsythe, speaking to the prone man and keeping his cold gaze unblinkingly upon Kathy. "All right, young lady," he went on, his voice changing again, becoming crisp with decision and authority. "If that's how you want to play I'll give you a choice. Burn this house to attract help—and your paw dies at the first puff of smoke. Old man, walk on out of here ahead of me.

Don't burn it and the old man lives. It's your choice to make."

Forsythe stepped back into the room, caught old Jared by the shoulder and brutally hurled him on out into the hallway where he barely escaped hurtling into Miranda. Forsythe then went out after Jared and turned once to show the others his ruthless eyes.

"Tonight'd be a real good night for a big fire, ma'am. Folks'd see it for twenty miles. You light it up any time you're a mind to—and I'll gut-shoot your paw, break both his legs at the knees, and give him back to you."

After Kathy, Miranda and Jack Carson were left alone the rangeboss said painfully through his broken mouth, "You tried, Kathy. No one can do any better."

But Miranda's opinion was different. "No good," she said severely. "You put your father in bad place. No good. Better you shouldn't have said anything. That bad man, he is getting worse every day. No good to cross him."

Kathy agreed with all this, with everything Miranda said, when she had a moment to think it over, and yet, like all the others, outlaws included, her temper was worn thin from the everlasting waiting, from the tension and unfriendliness. She sank gently down upon the side of Jack Carson's bed, looked at Miranda and Carson, waited until she heard the yonder front door open and close, then very softly said, "The marshal has set a trap. He knows Frank Canton rode towards Thunder Pass this morning. He also knows Canton is the only other outlaw who knows where those dynamite-bombs are hidden down in town."

"How do you know these things?" Carson mutteringly demanded.

"He slipped me a note when he was at the front door a while back, Jack. I burned it, but that's part of what it said."

"What else, Kathy?"

"That Marshal Belmont thinks he knows how to capture Forsythe's wild bunch without anyone but the outlaws getting hurt."

Carson groaned and rocked his head back and forth on the pillow, his eyes turning desperate as well as pained. "Kathy," he husked. "This is never going to work—any of it. Now Forsythe's got Jared too. Listen to me; you've got to get word to that Texas lawman to stay out of it; to let it run its natural course like your paw and I agreed to do."

"Jack, I can't," whispered Kathy. "I can't reach the marshal. There's no way. I can't even ride out any more. Forsythe won't let me. We've got to trust in Marshal Belmont."

"Yeah," muttered the rangeboss thickly. "An' get your paw killed sure as the devil!"

CHAPTER ELEVEN

AFTER night fell the main house with its three inhabitants was gloomy. Jack Carson got up, got dressed and went as far as the kitchen where he ate with Kathy and Miranda. None of them had much to say.

Over across the darkened yard an outlaw leaned casually upon a bunkhouse upright idly smoking and holding a Winchester saddle-gun in the bend of one elbow. This man from time to time looked northward as though listening. From the kitchen window Carson, Kathy and Miranda had no trouble figuring out that Forsythe's sentry was anxious for Frank Canton to return.

But Canton didn't come back. As the hours passed it appeared unlikely that he was going to ride on in. Later, Buck Forsythe himself took over the nightwatch. He alternated between gazing over at the main house and looking northeastward, the direction Canton would appear if he was coming at all.

Kathy began to worry and told Jack Carson she thought Marshal Belmont had apprehended Canton, and that if this were so, if Canton didn't return shortly, Forsythe would certainly suspect something.

Carson didn't agree. "Few men ride in the dark, Kathy, if they can find a place to unroll their bedroll. A cowboy can postpone a meal or two without any difficulty. Forsythe won't begin to get suspicious until tomorrow morning some time."

She had to be content with that, but just before retiring she walked out onto the gloomy porch. It was a pleasant night, warm and bell-clear and fragrant. The stars shone with their eternal brilliance, the sickle moon was growing fatter with the passing of the days, and somewhere far out a worried cow bawled softly for her strayed youngster.

Forsythe killed his smoke and turned to gaze over where Kathy stood faintly discernible, a rounded shadow against the housefront's weathered darkness. He seemed about to walk on over but he didn't. Instead he drew up a battered chair, sank down upon it and placed the carbine across his lap.

She returned to the house and found Miranda standing big-eyed in the parlour. Miranda was staring at her with fearful eyes. She didn't speak but she jerked her head and hiked on back through the pantry into the kitchen. Kathy followed.

Hyde Belmont was standing there well away from the window and the orange lamplight. She caught her breath at sight of him, stopped dead-still just inside the doorway and felt fear rise up from somewhere inside her and become almost a physical pain.

Belmont made a hand motion towards Miranda and said in Choctaw, "Take the light out into the parlour and put it on a table out there. In this place, I want only darkness."

Without a moment's hesitation Miranda moved to obey. As she passed along she said to Kathy in a swift whisper, "I told you he was a Sioux; look at his feet."

Kathy looked. Marshal Belmont didn't have his boots and spurs on, he was wearing ornate-tongued Dakota moccasins. He saw that look and smiled faintly.

"Everything people make is for some purpose. I had a lot of foot-work to do tonight and moccasins beat boots all hollow for walking silently."

He moved towards the table, lifted out a chair and sat down upon it. He motioned for Kathy to do the same across the table from him. It was shadowy now, in the huge old kitchen. Anyone happening along to look in couldn't make them out. In fact, when Miranda glided back to stand just inside the kitchen door and cross both arms across her chest, because her clothing was traditionally dark and her colouring blended, all Kathy could make out distinctly was Miranda's silhouette and the whites of her black eyes.

"Now I want some fast answers," said Belmont, not sounding in any hurry at all except in his crisp choice of words. "Who is the head man here with these outlaws?"

"He calls himself Buck Forsythe," replied Kathy quietly.

Belmont gently inclined his head. "He's not lying. That's his name. I thought it might be Forsythe. You see, every time I've got a look at those men of his—particularly the day they met you down in Thunder City—I've tried to place them. Finally I did—they are members of the wild bunch that runs with this Buck Forsythe. And yet, every time I've come out here—no Forsythe."

"He hides in the bunkhouse the minute he's warned of riders coming. He stands back in there with a carbine waiting and watching. The other day when you and Doctor Ford rode in, he had you squarely in the centre of a trap, Marshal."

"Big reward on Buck Forsythe," murmured Belmont. Then he turned brisk again, but Kathy spoke out ahead of him.

"Jack Carson and Forsythe had a fight today. Forsythe would have beaten Jack to death, but my father and I diverted him."

"Where's Carson now?"

"In one of our spare bedrooms. Miranda can get him if you—"

"No; never mind that for now. You can relay what I say to him. Now listen close, both of you. Those two cowboys I borrowed from the Kurt ranch today are serving as my deputies. One of them trailed Canton up to Thunder Pass. Canton's camped up there. He doesn't seem in any big hurry to get back."

Kathy could understand that but she said nothing to Marshal Belmont about the anxiety and tension which had been growing steadily more unpleasant as the days passed. What she said was: "If you arrest Frank Canton the others will know something has gone wrong."

Belmont leaned back, eyeing her steadily through the milky starlight. "Canton stays free as a bird. But let me warn you about him. I've wired the Texas and Kansas authorities for the correct names and the backgrounds of every man who rides with Buck Forsythe. Frank Canton is Forsythe's special assassin. Whatever you do, don't antagonise Canton."

"We know," stated Kathy, and explained about her father being taken as a hostage to the bunkhouse. Belmont listened, turned quietly thoughtful for a while afterwards, then he softly shrugged.

"You'd better get hold of yourself," he finally told her. "I can imagine how rough it's been. But by angering Forsythe you just might get killed. Take it for another day or two."

"What are you doing, Marshal? What plans have you made?"

"Some simple ones," he answered. "Forsythe is going

to see the signals from the Pass tomorrow or the next day. I'm not sure when we'll be ready to move because so far we've only found one more of those cussed dynamite clusters down in town. But the people are working hard day and night to get them all. I don't want anything to go wrong. If one of Forsythe's men manages to get away when we hit them—or if Forsythe gets suspicious and sends someone like Canton on ahead—or if, afterwards, when we get them all, someone else rides into town from the wild bunch and knows where those bombs are—getting Forsythe isn't going to compensate for losing half the town or the people in it . . . Or you folks, out here."

"I understand. Are you sure the coach will be here?"

He shook his head at her. "The bullion coach *won't* be here. In fact, Kathy, that particular coach has already bypassed Thunder City and is half way down towards Texas already. I wired for the federal marshals to re-route it. I've also wired for another coach to come southward through Thunder Pass, only this one will have armed deputies in it."

Kathy suddenly remembered something and pushed her next words out breathlessly. "That armed guard who works with Forsythe," she gasped. "The one riding with the other guards with that coach . . . !"

"Don't worry about him. Those were part of my instructions to the officers up north: Pick up each armed guard and hold them until it can be determined which man is the traitor."

Miranda said with strong approval. "You make good plan. You watch out for everything."

Belmont's level gaze drifted over to the squaw. His white teeth shone briefly in a small smile, it was a sardonic smile. "The plan is good enough to do what has to be done," he told Miranda. "Except for one thing—Thunder Pass Ranch. Forsythe will still have his hostages."

Miranda thought on this, then shrugged. In her fatalistic way she accepted the risks. Her shrug plainly said that this was how things had to be.

Belmont returned his attention to Kathy. "This troubles me," he said. "Especially if these men are edgy."

"They are," confirmed Kathy. "For the past week they've been getting more disagreeable; more anxious. I've even heard them snapping at one another."

"Then they'll shoot first and think afterwards," stated the Texas lawman. "And you folks will be right handy." He stood up without making a sound, looked down across the table at her and was briefly, thoughtfully quiet.

Miranda moved lightly to cross over to the stove where the big coffee pot stood. She knew the ways of rangemen and filled a cup with black java which she took over and offered the lanky Texan. He accepted the cup, muttered something Kathy didn't understand in that sliding, guttural tone, sipped for a moment then said, "I don't know what to tell you. I hope Forsythe'll use his hostages to buy his freedom with. I hope he'll be wise enough to realise it when he's whipped. But who knows what a desperate man will do? Maybe we can get between you folks and the outlaws over near the road. One thing you can rely on, Miss Kathy; whatever can be done will be done."

"You couldn't get between us if he takes us along," she told him. "The road is through our range eastward and there's no shelter out there; no trees or underbrush or rocks like there are back in the foothills."

Belmont put the cup down. "We're not going to hit him out in the open. The coach will break a wheel just before it leaves the foothills. I've already ridden around up there to pick the spot." He turned towards the back door, listened a moment then turned back to nod. But Kathy stood up when he moved noiselessly forward to trail after him, and at the yonder door she halted him with her fingers, went on past and boldly, quietly, passed on out first.

She stood for a moment looking and listening. The night was hushed and gloomy. She stepped back inside and told Miranda to look out the window over towards the bunkhouse. Miranda obeyed and afterwards drew a finger across her throat, then made the *wibluto* hand-sign for a chair. Forsythe the cut-throat, the killer, was still sitting over there on his chair.

Belmont stepped past Kathy out into the quiet night behind Jared Merritt's big old house. He paused to also test the night, then he turned back. Kathy was there watching him, her breathing shallow and her heart steadily beating. All it would take now would be for Forsythe to decide to walk once around the house. Forsythe might get killed, but so also would his unarmed prisoners. She put a hand lightly to the valley between her breasts.

Belmont, hesitating there beside her, slightly in front of

her, suddenly stepped even closer, suddenly dropped both hands to her hips and swayed her into him. She was too astonished to resist, to even understand immediately what was happening.

His gracefully curving hatbrim swooped down; his wide shoulders blacked-out the ancient stars, his lips sought and found her mouth. For an endless second she felt the quick, ragged breaking of his breath upon her cheeks, felt the hunger and the insistence of his mouth upon her lips, then she turned that one hand, pressed it to his chest and he released her, stepped back, turned and moved lithely away into the endless night.

She stood there for a full five minutes after Hyde Belmont was nowhere in sight; was still standing there when Miranda padded out to stand in the doorway looking straight at her with those inscrutable black eyes.

She turned, pushed past and re-entered the kitchen, went to the chair she'd vacated earlier and sat down again, placed both elbows on the table, put her chin in cupped hands and had nothing to say as Miranda also came back into the room speaking softly, saying Marshal Belmont was a man of powerful medicine, a Sioux among Sioux.

Eventually Miranda realised something had happened. She leaned upon her sink with crossed arms watching Kathy. Finally, deducing that whatever had occurred had not happened where she had seen it, Miranda ran some facts together and said, "What did he tell you out there?"

"Tell me?" murmured Kathy, shaking clear of her reverie to glance upwards. "He didn't tell me anything,

Miranda. He kissed me."

Miranda stiffened over where she stood. Her stare became fierce, but only for a moment, then it turned uncertain. Miranda had a hard judgment to make. She despised men; had ever since she'd been first married to one. But she also had a perplexing problem: She mightily respected Hyde Belmont the stalwart one—the Sioux—and there was something else which had been bothering her ever since Kathy had returned home. Kathy was at that ripe age; she had a duty to fulfil, a natural duty.

Miranda stood over there wrestling with her prejudice and her understanding of how the natural laws tugged and pulled, and in the end she didn't despise men any the less but she saw very clearly that *her* feelings were unlikely to have any effect upon the inevitable, so she wisely but brusquely said: "You would never go hungry with that one," which was close as she could drive herself to saying the tall Texan would be a suitable mate for her Kathy.

Then she loosened her arms, went to the stove and picked up the coffee pot, filled two cups, carried them both to the table and sat down. She and Kathy sipped bitter black liquid and eyed one another. There was nothing to say, really, so they were silent, this grim, fat Indian woman and the lithe, beautiful white girl she'd had a big hand in raising. They were, perhaps, separated by a thousand years of evolution in most things, but in one thing they were perfectly attuned: They were both females with all the ancient wisdom and intuition females possessed.

CHAPTER TWELVE

ACK CARSON listened with disbelief at what Kathy had to tell him the following morning at breakfast. He was aghast. He looked it and when he muttered he also sounded it.

"Why didn't one of you awaken me?" he asked Kathy. "I'd have liked to have talked to this Texas marshal."

"He said for us to tell you, Jack. We offered to get you up, but he was in a hurry. There wasn't time."

"Kathy; I got to think this over."

From the cook-stove old Miranda said. "Nothing to think over. This one acts. Not talk—acts."

Miranda's remark annoyed Carson. He scowled across the room but Miranda couldn't be touched by anything which caused as little physical hurt as a dark look. She went on serenely cooking breakfast.

Carson stopped eating, made a smoke and sat across the table playing with his full coffee cup and his cigarette while he considered piecemeal everything Kathy had told him. Finally he said, "One of us has got to keep a watch for those same signals Forsythe's watching for."

Kathy agreed with this.

Carson also said, "If he finds those darned bombs down in Thunder City that signal from the Pass will confirm that. Didn't he say he meant to find the bombs first—then send the coach along?"

Kathy nodded.

Carson got up. His face was just as battered and raw-looking as it had been the day before, but it seemed to bother him a lot less and also, much of the spring was back in his stride again as he crossed to the window and gazed out into the yard, his puffy eyes pinched down nearly closed.

"Somehow, we've got to tell your paw what's happening," he mused from over by the window.

"No tell," contradicted Miranda. "Only us know, only three chances others find out. More know, more bad chances."

There was of course good logic in Miranda's observation but it irritated Carson. He swung and fastened a baleful look over towards the stove.

Kathy stepped between those two and joined Jack at the window. Forsythe was out there in the yard, evidently talking to the man who had been on guard during the last night-watch. He and that other outlaw were speaking. Forsythe's back was towards Kathy's window but she could tell by his stance that Forsythe was in one of his evil moods.

At the bunkhouse, her father walked out looking rumpled but rested. The battered Missourian sauntered out with him. Jared looked at the sky and down lower, out across the empty rangeland where morning brightness was firming up already into a hard, bitter shine. He said something curt and the Missourian lifted his shoulders and dropped them, then Forsythe swung and started across where Jared and the Missourian were standing.

Jared also said something to Forsythe. The outlaw chieftain twisted to gaze over at the house. Kathy thought her father had asked permission to cross over. She held her breath; if this were so, and if Forsythe granted that wish, all her immediate worries would be over.

But Forsythe, when he turned back towards Jared, shook his head, growled something and her father turned about and walked back into the bunkhouse.

At Kathy's side where he'd also been watching all this, Jack Carson mildly swore under his breath and stalked on out into the parlour.

The morning wore along, its heat piling up out in the yard and eventually seeping into the house with sufficient intensity to make each of the people in there conscious of it. Idleness too plagued them. Without making any kind of formal arrangement they kept their vigil at the windows. A little after ten o'clock Buck Forsythe strolled over, got almost to the house, and was hailed by a relieved voice from the barn.

"Hey Buck—Frank's comin'."

Forsythe turned instantly and reversed his course. Kathy and Jack Carson, watching from a parlour window, saw the drag leave Forsythe's step, saw his shoulders roll up and his arms swing along as he headed back down towards the barn as though Forsythe was suddenly galvanised by strong hope.

Canton came walking his horse down into the yard. He swung off over at the barn, tossed his reins to that man down there who had first spied him, and stepped over to Forsythe. Kathy saw Canton wearily wag his head as he spoke; saw Forsythe's shoulders droop. Canton, she knew, had just reported no sighting of the bullion coach.

When Canton went on towards the bunkhouse, Buck

Forsythe stood a long time over beside the barn hitchrack. His expression was bitter and frustrated. He pushed around eventually and started over towards the house once again. Kathy, anticipating unpleasantness, said to Jack she thought he ought to go lie on his bed as though he were still suffering from his beating. Carson showed disapproval of this notion in his face, but he nevertheless departed from the parlour for the excellent reason that if Forsythe thought he was still incapacitated, Forsythe would ignore him for now.

When the outlaw chieftain stepped up onto the porch, reached for the latch and flung the door inward, Kathy was passing over towards the pantry door. She turned at his rough entrance and laid a level, cool look upon him.

Forsythe said to her, his eyes cold, "Why didn't you fire the place last night like you said you'd do?"

Her reply was cutting. "I didn't say I *would.* I only said I *could.*"

"But you didn't."

"Of course not. Not with my father in the bunkhouse with you and those others."

"He wants to talk to you. He asked me to let him come over here this morning."

"Well . . ."

"I got a better idea. You come along with me and talk to him over at the bunkhouse. But I don't know what you two've got to say unless you want to bawl on each other's shoulders."

Forsythe's mood was vicious, his eyes, the way they lay upon Kathy, were like ice. He had reached the complete end of his patience and showed it. As Hyde Belmont had said, this man and the men with him were totally deadly now. There had been too much frustration, too much waiting and disappointment and anxiety to be endured. Buck Forsythe and the other outlaws were not the kind of men who could stand being caged, whether by their own machinations or by the restrictive processes of others. They were violent, active, completely restless human beings.

"I don't know what we'd have to talk about," Kathy said coolly to him. "All I wish is that you'd get your signal that that bullion coach was on its way down the Pass."

Forsythe's dead-level gaze turned ironic. "You can't wish that nowhere near as much as I do. But all right; if you got nothing to say to Jared forget it. Just don't forget you're to stay in this—"

"Hey, Buck!"

That excited shout coming up through the dancing heat of the yard from the barn-area brought Forsythe around in a smooth, twisting turn. He went back out onto the porch, his eyes pinched nearly closed against the sunblast out there.

Two outlaws down at the barn were moving excitedly and pointing northeastward with rigid arms. Coming down from the broad notch in the yonder skyline were bitter-burning quick flashes of fierce bright light.

"The signal, Buck," one of those excited men at the barn called exultantly. "The damned signal! That lousy coach is finally comin'."

Forsythe stood stiff and erect for a half minute. Through

the door where she watched, Kathy got the distinct impression Forsythe's relief was enormous, that his mind was springing ahead to the fresh plans he must now evolve. She went over to the doorway and leaned there, but Forsythe didn't turn back, he instead stepped off the porch and went striding quickly ahead.

Kathy watched those white bursts of light from Thunder Pass. She didn't hear Miranda come up until the squaw said, "Things happen now."

Kathy saw the last ragged flash wink out, turned, and from the corner of her vision sighted Jack Carson standing back near the hallway entrance to the parlour. Jack had also caught those hard, dazzling bursts of light.

Kathy looked at them both and none of them spoke right away. In each of them excitement came to a quick head holding them silent, keeping them entirely occupied with their private thoughts for a while.

Out in the yard the outlaws came together up near the bunkhouse. Forsythe was giving crisp orders. Only Frank Canton seemed unperturbed; from time to time Canton gazed up at the Pass. It was as though Canton resented those signals arriving just as he'd abandoned hope of seeing them.

Jared walked on out onto the bunkhouse porch but no one paid him the slightest attention. He glanced up where Kathy stood near the doorway of the main house. He stepped down into the bitter heat and Forsythe saw him over there. For a second the outlaw leader paused, then he raised his voice.

"Merritt; go fetch your girl, Carson—if he's able—and

that damned Injun. Fetch 'em down to the barn. The lot of you are goin' with us. Shake a leg, old man!"

Jared turned and struck out instantly for the house. Kathy saw him coming and waited, still eyeing those excited outlaws out there who seemed now to have quite forgotten their endless, nerve-wracking weeks of waiting, and even the searing summer sunlight which was coming down upon them in searing waves.

The moment her father stepped inside Kathy closed the door and rushed quick, blunt words at him. Jared looked and listened, and very gradually as Kathy recounted all that she knew, his faded eyes grew wider. Finally he said in a husky, incredulous way: "You mean that Texas marshal's found the last of Forsythe's bombs?"

"He said he wouldn't put the rest of his plan into execution until he'd found them all," replied Kathy.

Old Jared twisted to gaze over at Jack Carson. The rangeboss gazed straight back. These two were suddenly faced with the fact that although they'd both grimly played out their pre-arranged game with Forsythe, Kathy's coming home had twisted the entire thing out of focus; now, instead of being prime movers in the counter-plot against Forsythe's wild bunch, they were now only of secondary importance. Kathy and Marshal Belmont were the key figures.

Jared worked up a little sardonic grin and Carson did the same right back at him. Carson said, "Jared; the Lord takes care of fools, babies and drunks—which are we?"

"Fools maybe," answered the old cowman. "But I never felt better about bein' one in my life. And all the suspi-

cions I've been havin' about that Texas lawman. . . ."
Jared wagged his head back and forth.

Miranda suddenly projected herself into this exchange by producing from inside her loose-fitting dress somewhere, three razor-sharp skinning knives which she held out to them. "No guns—these next best," she pronounced, and waited throughout the long silence while Kathy, her father, and Jack Carson considered those wicked implements. "Better to go with knives than with nothing," Miranda said stonily, pushed a slightly curved, bitter-shining and freshly honed knife into Kathy's unresisting hand. "Put it in your boot. Knife plenty good for woman. Put it away."

They took the knives, none of them doing so with any great show of enthusiasm, but each of them aware that Miranda's blunt logic was infallible. Even a skinning-knife under the circumstances was better than no weapon at all. It was Jack Carson who spoke for the three of them when he dryly said, "Never had much use for these things but Miranda's right—beggars can't be choosers."

They hid the knives and looked solemnly at each other. If the crisis had arrived for their captors, it had also arrived for them. They knew exactly what Forsythe meant to use them for, and at least two of them had grim misgivings about what fate afterwards awaited them, but nothing was said of this except when Jared mumbled something about the trail ahead being a rough one for them at the very best.

Out in the yard the outlaws were feverishly saddling their horses. When they'd completed rigging out their own animals they returned to rope and lead forth another four horses. These beasts they also went to work upon, and as the others did this Buck Forsythe turned, gazed over at the house, straightened fully around eventually and started on towards the place where four sets of grim faces watched his approach.

Kathy said, "Dad—Jack: Please; don't do anything to anger them. You've proven all you have to prove and if the people of Thunder City ever have anyone to thank for saving their town as well as their lives, it's you two. So please. . . ."

Forsythe's solid step struck hard down upon the yonder porch causing her to let the rest of whatever admonition she was going to pronounce, die out into deep silence.

Forsythe filled the doorway. He gazed around at them all; gazed longest at Jack Carson. He said, speaking directly to Jack, "Thought you might still be flat on your back, cowboy. Figured I might have to send Frank Canton in here to salt you down." Forsythe paused to speculatively consider Carson. "May have to do it yet. If you're not up to a long hard ride we can't have you left behind or slowin' us down."

"I can keep up with you or anyone else," Carson replied thinly, his battered, swollen features showing their firm dislike.

Forsythe nodded and dropped his gaze to Kathy. The coldness was still there in his eyes, but there was something more alive, more full of alert feeling, in his gaze now too. This was the kind of moment Buck Forsythe lived for; this period of feverish activity and fierce anticipation. She could even imagine him smiling now.

He said: "All of you will ride with us to the robbery. Don't try to run off—you can't out-run a bullet on those cowhorses you'll be astride. And don't try anything else foolish either. If you behave right smart, maybe you'll live through this. Remember that, every time you think of something else. Now come on; we've got a lot of ground to cover and not a whole lot of time to cover it in. Move out!"

They left the house ahead of Forsythe bound straight down where the impatient outlaws were waiting with the horses. Sunlight burnt against them, the heat danced all around, and far off where the mountains stood highest, there was a soft-blurred haze over everything.

Miranda snarled when a man stepped up to give her a boost into the saddle. One of the other outlaws laughed as his companions recoiled backwards from that snarl. Forsythe, turning to see, almost smiled. The only man among those bandits who acted exactly as he'd always acted was Frank Canton the killer. Canton put a slow, thoughtful glance over at Miranda, stepped up across his saddle and ran that same chilling look over their other hostages, letting it lie longest upon Kathy.

They rode out of the yard behind Buck Forsythe, and dust jerked to life beneath their horses' hooves. Forsythe loped out on his big bay thoroughbred and could handily have left them far back in a twinkling had he not impatiently held the thoroughbred in. All the horses were fresh though, and until sweat darkened their coats Forsythe let them run on. But he slowed as they swept around a rolling rib of land and sighted the stageroad a couple of miles ahead. He had no intention of doing what he'd set his mind to, riding run-out horses.

Frank Canton rode beside Kathy but he never once looked around at her. The other outlaws remained sagely behind Jack and Jared and profusely perspiring Miranda. There was no possible way for any of the hostages to make a break for it.

CHAPTER THIRTEEN

THEY got close enough to the stageroad for the outlaws to begin a critical study of the up-country trace where the road came angling down from high up and farther back. But that northward country was shaded and darkened by trees and brush. The only way to determine accurately that the coach would be coming along up there was by hearing its approach.

Forsythe halted and sat perfectly still, gazing off northward. When the others of his party did the same Forsythe's brows gradually drew darkly down. His men came to also slowly scowl; there wasn't a sound coming from farther back up Thunder Pass.

Frank Canton said quietly: "Buck; something's wrong."

Kathy held her breath. She didn't dare square around to look at either Jack Carson or Miranda. She knew what had supposedly happened back up there in the hidden places of Thunder Pass: The coach had broken a wheel.

Forsythe jerked his head at Canton. "Go have a look,"

he growled. "And be careful."

As Canton reined away in a loose lope Forsythe twisted to gaze at the prisoners. Lest her expression betray her Kathy swung to watch Canton grow small where he crossed open country towards the lifting hills and their dark green covering.

The Missourian said, "I hope they're broke down. That's a lousy road up in there."

No one else said anything.

The sun burned fiercely, their horses stood head-hung under the pressure of that heat, sweating right where they stood. Forsythe removed his hat, wiped a sleeve across his forehead and dropped the hat back down again. He eased his well-worn .45 in and out of its smooth holster. He was uncertain, Kathy saw, and wary.

Jared, who wore a coat summer and winter, felt around in his pockets, found some tobacco, some papers, and started to make a smoke. He was only an indifferent smoker, and right then he actually felt no compulsive need for that cigarette, but this waiting was making his nerves crawl. When he lit up the Missourian held forth his left hand with an ingratiating smile. Jared handed over the makings.

They went on waiting out there under the bitter sun, their discomfort increasing. All but Miranda showed distinct uneasiness and wire-tight tension. She sat stolidly up there across her saddle looking indifferently from the puffing Missourian to his companions. She looked longest at Forsythe's broad back up ahead of her. It took no great powers of divination to guess old Miranda's thoughts; she was considering Forsythe's broad, heavy shoulders as an excellent place to bury that knife to the hilt which she had concealed somewhere beneath her shapeless old dress.

They were back several hundred yards from the stageroad with an excellent view all around, but clearly, in the minds of Forsythe and his outlaw-band, this glaring exposure was not what they wished. Anyone coming in any direction could see them sitting out there.

But no one came until Frank Canton came loping back nearly an hour later when all of them, even the prisoners, were beginning to wilt from the shimmering heat.

Canton threw a casual glance at the others and said to Buck Forsythe, "They're up there all right. Two fellers off the coach—driver and swamper—and the three guards."

"Did you see Hiram?" asked Forsythe, evidently referring to the outlaw who was riding with this supposed bullion coach as one of the armed guards.

Canton shrugged. "I didn't get that close. They stopped with a busted wheel or a busted axle, one or the other, atop a little rise in the road where there's open ground for five acres in every direction. I didn't das't get too close."

"Busted axle?" said the Missourian from around the cigarette between his lips. "Hell; we got all day to do this then. They couldn't be carryin' a spare an' the closest new axle would be down at Thunder City." He killed his smoke on the saddlehorn and tossed it away. "What d'you say, Buck?"

Forsythe said shortly, "You shut up an' let me do the thinkin'."

The Missourian subsided and Canton swung for a look roundabout. The land was empty as far as anyone could see. It was now close to midday, which was fortunate for the outlaws because in the summertime Southwest no one rode out in midday unless their business was extremely urgent. It was too hard on men and also on horses.

"Clear all around," Canton murmured, coming back to gaze at Forsythe.

The outlaw leader was looking thoughtfully northward up towards the inviting shade where the trees and hills began. He made a motion with his head.

"Lead off, Frank, and be damned careful. We'll get one good, clean chance at them. If we muff that there's going to be a fight an' while the folks down in Thunder City may not hear the shootin', those fellers still equal us in numbers even without countin' Hiram."

Canton looked slightly saturnine when he said, "Buck; ain't no one got an even chance when we got the drop."

They followed Canton northward towards the trees. The Missourian was softly smiling, but his eyes were speculative as though he were balancing their chances if a fight should start.

Kathy and Miranda exchanged a sliding glance as they passed along. Jack Carson and old Jared rode side by side with one of the outlaws directly behind them. They could neither speak nor dare give each other a knowing look because of this renegade's constant watchfulness.

Where the forest began it turned less burning but the heat was just as oppressive, and it was breathless in among the motionless, stiff-standing trees. Canton had just pioneered his way up through here so the trail was fresh in his mind; he rode along as though he were an old hand in this place.

Kathy tried to visualise those men with the stalled coach as she rode. Clearly, since Canton had reported a driver, a swamper, and three armed guards, the men who had been secreted inside the stage had jumped out the moment the thing had halted and had hidden themselves in the under-brush close by.

What heightened her fear and her dread was that when the fight began, she and the others with her would be caught in the same devastating fire which would be directed at their captors. Her only hope, and she clung to it stubbornly, was Marshal Belmont; he also knew the peril the hostages would be in. He would have warned those gunmen up ahead.

She rode with her gaze constantly searching the underbrush, the tree-shadows, the dozens of gloomy places men could hide in ambush, hoping against hope that Hyde Belmont would show himself to her. He never did.

Frank Canton halted deep in the forest, stepped down, unshipped his booted Winchester and stood there while the others also alighted. He said quietly to Forsythe, "Straight off through the trees there about a half mile. That's where they're workin' on the coach, Buck. You can't hear 'em from here—but neither can they hear us."

Canton looked around. "Leave someone here to watch the hostages an' let's go."

If Forsythe noticed Canton doing the same thing he'd growled at the Missourian for—telling him what to do—he gave no sign of it. He turned, looked at the bunched-up prisoners and bobbed his head at one of the dismounted outlaws also standing back there. "You stay," he ordered. "Keep a close watch too, and not just on these people; on our horses too."

Forsythe, Canton, and the Missourian started off through the trees, their footfalls deadened by an ancient, springy pine-needle and leafmould carpet.

The man left to keep watch walked back twenty feet and planted his thin shoulders against a big tree. He was young and clear-eyed and had the pointed-chinned face of a ferret. He alternately watched Jack Carson and Kathy. Old Miranda and Kathy's father didn't seem to this outlaw to warrant much consideration.

Kathy turned and quietly said, "You wouldn't think of selling out for a hundred dollars, would you?"

The outlaw shook his head. "You don't have enough money to compare with my share off that bullion coach, lady. If you live to be a thousand you won't have that kind of money."

Obviously, their guard was concentrating all his thoughts on what was shortly to be his.

Old Jared twisted to say, "Money's no earthly good to a dead man, young feller. A man'd be a sight better off with a hundred in his pockets than an ounce of lead through his heart."

The outlaw mirthlessly smiled at old Jared. "Forget it,"

he exclaimed. "I've waited too long. Anyway, nothing's going to happen. But even if it did—even if there's a fight—we still got all the advantage. As for that ounce of lead, oldtimer, hell, I'd gamble *that* kind of money against a bullet any day."

Jared turned his back on the outlaw. He eyed Kathy with a wry expression and removed his hat to mop off sweat. Jack Carson's raw face was turning bright red from fresh sunburn. From time to time Jack grimaced. He was in pain. Not only from his face but also from his cracked ribs and his sore stomach muscles. He stepped over to a tree and eased down, but for all this seeming concentration upon his own welfare to the exclusion of all else, Kathy noticed that Carson had squatted in such a way that all he had to do was roll sideways and that tree would be between him and their guard.

Miranda stood like a dark-hued statue. She was listening. Kathy knew Miranda's hearing was far more acute than the hearing of the others. She never took her eyes off Miranda for as long as the minutes slipped by. If anything happened out there Miranda would know it seconds before the others did; when Miranda moved Kathy meant to also move.

"What the hell's takin' 'em so long," the outlaw guard growled, and fidgeted over where he stood.

Carson had a reasonable answer to that. "You heard what Canton said; even with that Judas among those fellers, they still equal you in numbers. If Forsythe is smart he'll take his time and plenty of it to get into position before he calls out."

Kathy, glancing from Miranda over at their guard, suddenly saw something faintly move then fade out behind the guard perhaps fifty yards off. She caught her breath, dropped her head swiftly so that the startlement wouldn't be seen, then very gradually raised her head and threw a careless look out through the gloomy forest again.

But there was nothing more to be seen out there.

She tried to minutely recall that movement and failed. It could have been an animal, perhaps a deer fading out from the scent of people. It could even have been a little clump of falling leaves. It had only very briefly moved at all.

Then too, it could have been Marshal Belmont; he was surely up in here somewhere, and whatever had made that quick, shadowy move hadn't made a sound. The last time she'd seen Hyde Belmont he hadn't made a sound either.

Kathy was hoarding her secret thoughts so intently that for a moment she neglected to notice that Miranda had casually turned to also gaze over past their guard where that vague, shadowy motion had appeared.

The guard, believing Miranda was watching him, said, "Injun; you get any funny ideas an' I'll bust your damned head like a rotten melon. What you starin' at anyway?"

Miranda turned her head, set her broad back squarely to that outlaw and crossed both arms over her ample chest. She didn't answer him. In fact, so far as she was now indicating, that man back there didn't exist at all.

But Kathy saw Miranda's black eyes come around to her, saw them straining to convey a meaning. Kathy was relieved. That *hadn't* been an illusion then. Miranda had also seen it.

The guard shifted position, left his rearward tree and strolled up closer to his prisoners. He dropped his right hand to let it lightly lie upon the holstered forty-five lashed to his right hip. He was patently becoming uneasy. They had all of them been standing there quiet and more or less motionless for nearly fifteen minutes now. All those long weeks of deadly waiting had played havoc with this man's nerves. These past fifteen minutes had brought all that to a head. As the man had intimated, he was at long last within moments of achieving great wealth. Every dragging second was an eternity. Each exhaled breath put him closer to something—to heady success or something else. Right now he was very clearly concerned with the 'something else'.

"What the hell's goin' on up there," he snarled.

Kathy attempted to soothe him by saying, "If it's quiet there's been no trouble. I wish they'd come back too."

The outlaw slumped a little but his gun-hand remained within inches of that loaded .45.

CHAPTER FOURTEEN

ROM the eastward forest Buck Forsythe suddenly stepped forth. His unexpected appearance was so abrupt it even brought the guard's .45 half out of leather. They all turned to see, and Kathy's heart sank. Forsythe's face was sweat-shiny and wire-tight. He pushed through the hostages and said to the guard gruffly, "It's the damned off-wheel. We've been waitin' for them to come around on our side of that lousy coach."

"I wondered," murmured the younger outlaw.

"It's no good, all this waitin'."

"Slip northward," suggested the younger man, "then get across the lousy road an' come in behind 'em."

"Better yet," snapped Forsythe, turning to glare at the hostages. "We make them come to us. You watch those two women. I'll watch the men and we'll drive these people up where Frank's waiting. They're hostages so by gawd we'll use 'em as hostages. We'll let those fellers see 'em and get 'em around on our side of that damned coach."

Forsythe was frustrated and furious. He didn't allow his companion to speak, he motioned with his gun-hand for the prisoners to walk ahead. He said, looking particularly at old Miranda, "Don't try slippin' off in the trees. Don't try anything cute at all; your lousy lives are hangin' by a hair right now. Walk straight ahead and don't any of you make a cussed sound. *Not one sound!*"

Kathy, looking past those two renegades, saw movement out there again, but much closer than she'd seen it earlier. She didn't face around when the others did, to walk ahead as Forsythe had ordered. She waited with desperate hope right up to the last second, then Forsythe drew his .45 and cocked it.

"I'll kill you as sure as I'm standing here," Forsythe told her softly.

Behind him fifteen yards back she saw that stalking noiseless shape firm up beside a tall tree. It was Hyde Belmont exactly as she'd prayed it might be, and he had his sixgun up and ready, but he became absolutely silent and motionless at sight of Forsythe's cocked gun pointed at her. He didn't dare make a move. Kathy understood. She turned and walked along behind her father and Jack Carson. She had difficulty breathing and this wasn't entirely attributable to the stillness of the thin mountain air.

Canton and that other outlaw raised up suddenly from off to the right, beckoned the captives towards them, looked frowningly at Forsythe and shook their heads, evidently to indicate there was no change in the onward situation.

Out through the yonder trees where the sunblast lay like a pewter curse over a naked old roadway, stood that battered, dusty coach. From the far side of it came the sounds of men's voices, sometimes grunting as though under strain, sometimes garrulously complaining about their exposure to the scalding sun.

It was a natural scene, Kathy thought, when she stepped in beside Frank Canton with Miranda and halted where Canton growled at them; it was hard not to believe the coach actually didn't have a broken wheel.

Canton said very softly, "The four of you stand right where you are." He then leaned over towards Forsythe and growled, "All right; walk up a ways an' make your play, Buck. I'm getting tired of all this. By gawd I never seen a job where everything went wrong like it has with this job."

The youthful outlaw, standing back a foot behind Forsythe and straining forward to see the coach out there through the trees, ran a long, tight sigh past his closed lips. Then he straightened up and drew his sixgun. When he turned half around so that Kathy had a view of his face, this man was faintly smiling. None of the other outlaws were, not even the Missourian who usually had a habitual grin around his lips. He was squatting behind a greeny old boulder which was fuzzed-over with mottled lichen. He too had his gun up and ready, but this time it was a Winchester carbine pointed on through the trees, instead of a .45.

Forsythe cast a final look around, found the hostages ringed round by his men, found also that his captives were pale and tense, and stepped ahead through the trees bound onward for the roadside or at least as far as the last tree-fringe.

Kathy slowly turned and slowly ran a rummaging look behind, back the way they had come up here near the road. If she expected to see Hyde Belmont again she was disappointed. There was nothing behind them but the silent trees and the mottled, deep shadows of this breathless place.

The complete stillness was abruptly broken by Forsythe's needlessly loud shout. It bounced off tree-trunks, off the close-by hillsides, and its booming echo went endlessly off through the surrounding countryside.

"You fellers with the coach—step around to the west side."

Kathy and all the others were caught up and held by the onward drama which they could only imperfectly see through the trees. No one paid any attention to the rearward forest for these tense minutes.

Four men sauntered around the coach to stand out there dripping sweat, gazing over where Forsythe had shouted from. One of those men was grey, grizzled, and looked rock-hard in the face. The others were younger men but with identical expressions of unrelenting opposition.

"Yeah," growled that tough-looking, rugged older man, his tone unfriendly. "What d'you want an' who are you? Step out where I can see you, mister."

Forsythe didn't do that; he remained back among the trees, but he told them what they had to know. "My name's Buck Forsythe an' maybe you've heard of me. Where's the fifth man?"

"What fifth man?" asked that fearless, greying man with a contemptuous ring to his words.

"Mister," snarled Forsythe, "you're under a lot of guns from back in these lousy trees; you go on playin' games and talkin' hard and you're goin' to wind up dead. You know damned well what fifth man I'm talkin' about. That other armed guard."

"Oh him," rumbled the spokesman for those four capable looking, rumpled men over beside their coach. "He's still around back." The greying man swung his head and called. At once another stalwart cowboy strolled on around into plain sight.

Beside Kathy but lower down where he hunkered, the Missourian gasped and said, "Hell, that ain't *him*. What's goin' on here?"

Although that tough-looking older man out there couldn't possibly have heard this remark, when next he spoke to Buck Forsythe he answered it.

"You expectin' someone else, Mister Forsythe? You fig-urin' maybe there'd be someone here you knew?"

Kathy held her breath. Forsythe didn't answer for a long time and she was afraid for those five men out there in front of their coach.

"You caught him," Forsythe said, making a statement of that. "All right; Hiram never was very smart anyway. But that don't change anything. Open that coach and put the bullion boxes out in the roadway."

One of those armed and rough-looking strangers out there turned and started to open a door, but his com-panion said, "Hold it just a minute," and peered over into the trees where Forsythe's voice was coming from. "Hell," he said disgustedly, "I'd always heard this here Buck Forsythe was a reg'lar terror. You know what I'm beginnin' to think; I'm beginnin' to think that there feller skulkin' over yonder in the trees is just some two-bit punk who's went and borrowed Forsythe's name, because if that really was Forsythe, he wouldn't be too yellow to show himself. Just leave them boxes in the coach."

Frank Canton stepped away from his shielding tree and raised his Winchester, squinted, lowered it and manoeuvred around through the trees to where he might get a good aim. As he did this Forsythe swore fiercely at those exposed men out in the bitter-burning roadway and ordered them to throw away their guns.

Canton stepped upon a dry twig that loudly snapped. Every head whipped towards that give-away sharp sound in the otherwise stillness and Canton jumped clear as though he'd been stung, lit down ten feet distant and, throwing caution to the wind, tramped on up where Forsythe stood. He raised his carbine again. Kathy, who was watching Canton along with all the others, was sure he meant to shoot down that grizzled man out there, and probably Canton did, but the man started speaking again, directing his remarks to Buck Forsythe who remained hidden.

"Want to know what happened to Hiram, Mister Forsythe? Want to know why I'm goin' to make you earn every red cent you take off this coach? Because Hiram's in jail over at Guthrie—and because he told us you'd be waitin' along here somewhere to take the bullion boxes."

Forsythe put up an arm to restrain Canton from shooting. He was staring hard at that grizzled man out there. Buck Forsythe, like all the successful men of his trade, had a highly-developed sixth-sense. Right now he had a bad feeling about all this and it kept increasing the longer he stood there.

He murmured, "Wait a minute, Frank. Something's going on here." He lowered that restraining arm and called forth again to those five fearless men out in the roadway. "Keep talkin', mister. What's the rest of it?"

"You really want to know, Forsythe? All right, I'll tell you. You thought when the bunch of us walked right on around where you could cover us you'd won, didn't you? Well; there are five hidden guns aimed right at the sound of your voice from the east side of the road—and there is a posse from Thunder City behind you back there in them trees. Marshal Hyde Belmont's in charge of that Thunder City posse and he's got twelve men back there with him cutting off your retreat. Now then, you wanted some answers an' you got 'em. From now on whatever happens it's squarely up to you. What say Forsythe; you want to fish or cut bait?"

Forsythe snarled: "You're a damned liar. If you had that kind of fire-power, mister, you'd have opened up long ago."

"Wrong again," rumbled the grizzled man, and altered his grim tone briefly to say, with a wag of his head. "I'll be switched, Forsythe. I had you figured for a lot tougher an' smarter man than you're turnin' out to be. Hell; we don't figure to open up on you and your pardners—not until you either open up on us, or until you refuse to hand over them hostages you got with you."

For a long interval of silence no one said anything. Those men out there with their pinched-down eyes and hatbrim-shaded bronzed faces, looked death squarely in the face and were contemptuous of it. Even cold-blooded Frank Canton lowered his gun to study those men, to slowly turn over in his mind what their leader had said.

Forsythe turned to Canton. "They did it. I don't know how but those people from Thunder Pass Ranch got word outside what we were up to."

But Canton shook his head, looking bitterly out into the roadway. "That damned Hiram," he growled. "Wait until I get that yellow-bellied traitor in my sights. They banged on him a little and he told 'em everything he knew. I'll kill him a little at a time startin' with both knees an' workin' upwards."

Forsythe twisted fully around to look back through the

gloomy trees. Kathy couldn't make out his expression but she had no trouble reading meaning into the way Forsythe was standing; he was badly shaken. He was fearful and desperate.

"Hey, Forsythe," called out that grizzled man from over by the coach. "You want these here bullion boxes? Just send them hostages out and we'll start unloadin'."

Canton snarled. "You damned liar. If you knew all about us they'd never have let you bring the bullion along."

The grizzled man started to shrug about this. He may even have been on the point of answering up, but from behind the outlaws Marshal Belmont's unmistakable quiet Texas drawl spoke first.

Belmont said, "Forsythe; the bullion boxes aren't worth the lives of those hostages you've got. What that man out there just told you is the gospel truth, every word of it. You're completely surrounded; you can't fight clear and you sure-'nough aren't going to talk your way clear. You've got just one chance—trade the hostages for the bullion boxes. Either that, or die where you're standin'."

"Yeah?" snarled Frank Canton. "You fire just one shot, lawman, an' I'll start the massacre. I'll kill the old man, then his rangeboss, then that damned squaw an' finally, I'll gut-shoot the girl."

Belmont's voice addressed Forsythe again ignoring Canton. It was the same cool, perfectly normal quiet drawl too. "Forsythe; killing the hostages—even winging 'em—will guarantee your own death and the death of every man with you. I give you my solemn word on that.

Now you've got one minute, Forsythe: Take the bullion boxes and give us the hostages and take your chances on escaping. Or start shooting."

Frank Canton would have squared fully around with his raised Winchester but this time Forsythe moved first. "Damn you, Frank," he swore. "Use what little brains you were born with." He gave Canton a rough shove back towards where the other brace of outlaws were sweating, where Kathy and the other hostages were listening and watching, white to the eyes. What all these opposing men were arguing about so savagely, was their lives.

The Missourian jumped up the second Canton and Forsythe appeared. His shirt was dark with perspiration. He said, "Make the trade, Buck, make the trade. We figured there might be trouble. Maybe not quite like this, but trouble all the same. The important thing is the bullion. If they're crazy enough to figure four stinkin' lives are worth all that money, why then we—"

"Yeah?" snarled Forsythe. "And how do we afterwards get away, you idiot? You heard where Belmont was talkin' from—him and that Thunder City posse with him is between us and our horses."

The youthful renegade said swiftly, "Take the coach, Buck. Sure; I know it won't be near' as good for us to get away in as our horses, but I been squattin' here doin' some arithmetic. You got any idea how many guns they got against us? By my cal'clations—twenty-two or twenty-three. Buck; can't no horses in the world out-run that many bullets, specially loaded down with that bullion. But—that damned coach'll give us all the protection we need, from inside it."

Frank Canton, Forsythe and the Missourian stared at the youngest outlaw. The hostages too looked over at that younger man. Jared said gruffly, "The only sense any of you have made so far has just been spoken."

Canton whirled savagely on Kathy's father but Forsythe snapped at him and Frank only glared. But the knuckles gripping his carbine, Kathy saw, were white from wrathful straining.

Forsythe said with a little brisk nod, "That's it. We'll make them give us an hour start."

"They won't do it," growled Canton. "And even if they promised, I wouldn't believe a damned one of 'em."

"They'd do it if we took one of 'em along and give 'em the others for that bullion, Frank," stated Forsythe, and looked from face to face among his men. Even Frank Canton, after considering this for a moment, appeared to favour it. Forsythe jerked his head at the hostages. "Come on up by the road."

Old Jared stood fast. "Which one goes with you?" he demanded.

Forsythe ranged a thoughtful look around before saying, "Kathy; she'd be double-insurance. We could kill you and it wouldn't stop 'em, but no one likes seein' a pretty girl dyin' from a gut-shot. Now move on up."

CHAPTER FIFTEEN

UCK FORSYTHE made his offer. He would, he called out, trade Carson, Miranda and old Jared for the coach with the bullion boxes in it.

Belmont called forth from back behind the troubled outlaws. "You forgot one hostage, Forsythe."

"I didn't forget her, lawman. She goes with us to make danged sure you don't follow. We could give her to you an' take your promise about an hour's lead—but Frank doesn't think your word's any good—so she goes along."

"No soap," growled that bass-voiced, grizzled battler from out in the roadway. "All the hostages or none. You're gettin' the coach and the boxes—you got to take some chances, Forsythe."

But Hyde Belmont over-rode this. "Forsythe; suppose *I* go with you instead of Kathy?"

Forsythe, Kathy saw, suddenly began to look enormously relieved. He had correctly read into the Texan's offer a willingness to parley instead of opening up on the bandits.

"Like your friend just said, Belmont—no soap. The girl goes with us. We won't harm her unless you push for a fight. We'll turn her loose wherever we abandon the coach."

From the roadway that grizzled man, after a moment of thought, said, "Forsythe; suppose we give you your horses and the bullion."

Frank Canton called that grizzled man an unprintable

name. "Why? So you can volley-fire after we're headin' out?"

The grizzled man's answer was curt and angry. That cursing had evidently put him on the verge of violence. "If you had a lick o' sense you'd know we wouldn't das't do that with the girl ridin' along."

Forsythe and Canton exchanged a look. It was tempting, this offer of their horses, but once more that younger outlaw spoke up to dampen the enthusiasm of Canton and Forsythe.

"They've had plenty of time to yank off the shoes and otherwise tamper with our horses back there. Don't trust 'em, Buck."

Forsythe nodded and turned back towards the roadway. "Take it or leave it," he shouted. "The girl goes with us in the coach, an' you fellers can have the squaw, Jack Carson and old man Merritt. You got ten seconds to spit or close the window."

For the first time since this heated exchange had begun, Kathy spoke up. She turned and called out: "Marshal Belmont? This is Katherine Merritt. I'll go with them in the stage. Please do as I ask: Take care of Jack and Miranda and my father." She turned, saw the steady eyes of all those people with her watching, and called ahead to the five bitter-faced men over by the coach. "We're coming out; don't touch your guns and please walk away from the coach."

No one moved out there in the road. No one spoke from behind, back in the forest. This heavy silence ran on and on. Forsythe smiled with his lips in a wolfish way. In a near-whisper he said, "Girl; you've got what I like—guts."

Even the Missourian was smiling again, his vacant smile, and Frank Canton was stonily regarding her with something close to respect—at least as close to respect as a cold-blooded killer like Canton could show, or even understand. It was the younger outlaw who said, "Ma'am; step out of the trees to the edge of the roadway an' let's just see what them buzzards out there figure to do."

She glanced at Buck Forsythe and he faintly nodded. She stepped forward to the last tree-fringe, paused to study those rugged, dark and shadowed faces out there, sucked in a big breath and moved straight out into the brilliant, fierce sunlight where she was in plain sight.

Those five men at the coach looked and said nothing. They were like men turned to stone. There wasn't a sound anywhere. She turned to beckon one of the outlaws forward behind her, and found that younger one already there. "Tell 'em to get away from the coach," he hissed. She obeyed and those men out there did as she asked, but with very great reluctance. They had never obeyed that order from Buck Forsythe to discard their guns, and now several of them let their right hands lie gently upon pistol-butts.

Canton jumped out of the forest into bitter brightness with his cocked Winchester held purposefully low. He didn't say a word but each of those men near the coach withdrew their gun-hands. Then and not until then, Canton said softly over his shoulder: "All right; let's go."

But Forsythe herded the other hostages out when he and the Missourian came forth. These two carefully kept their prisoners between them and those bitter-eyed men standing twenty feet away from the stage. The Missourian repeated Forsythe's earlier command.

"Throw down them guns!"

That grizzled, older man, glaringly replied to this. "Throw down nothin'. You got the coach and the boxes that's all you're goin' to get!"

Forsythe didn't insist; he instead called out for the younger outlaw to run around and make dead-certain that wheel was ready to roll. After this inspection had been made the younger man stepped over by the nearside door and frowned over at Buck.

"Nothin' wrong with that wheel I could see. Maybe it was the—"

"Never mind," snapped Forsythe, keeping his full attention about the five men northward up the road. "Open that damned door. I want to see those bullion boxes."

The younger man wrenched the door open, peered in, ran his breath out in a sharply audible fashion and stepped back so the others could also see four steel-bound oaken bullion boxes on the floor of the coach. The Missourian smiled broadly and flung sweat off his chin with a quick jerk.

"I'll check the teams and harness," he said. "Don't quite trust them fellers up the road there; 'pears to me they're too blessed clever for their own damned good."

Forsythe and the other outlaws kept their hostages in front and around them. They knew Marshal Belmont and his possemen from Thunder City were behind them. They also knew as long as they kept their hair-triggered guns cocked and pressed lightly into the unresisting flesh of those hostages, neither Belmont nor anyone else in opposition to them would dare interfere or dare to fire a single shot.

The Missourian sang out: "Horses and gear are fine. Buck; let's get to rollin'." As he said this the Missourian started hand over hand up the far side of the coach to the high overhead seat where the lines were looped around the tight-set wheel-brake.

Forsythe's shirtfront was limp and dark with sweat. Those five men up the road were concentrating their full, deadly intention upon him to the exclusion of all the others. He moved carefully forward until he was directly behind Kathy, pushed his pistol-barrel into her yielding flesh and growled: "Get in the coach!"

Those shadowy wraiths from Thunder City finally appeared through the forest, came out to the edge of the road and halted. If Forsythe and his outlaws had ever had doubts about the posse they could now see clearly that it was very real and very lethal. Hyde Belmont stood in the forefront completely away from the trees, his sixgun holstered, his steady gaze hard upon the coach as Kathy climbed in, scrambled over the boxes and was instantly followed by the youngest renegade, and finally by Buck Forsythe himself.

As Forsythe closed the coach door he pushed his head through to swing a hostile scowl from the men up the road over to Belmont's posse. As he did this more men walked out of the forest. These latter men, five in number, had rifles in their hands. They obviously were the others who had come south with the coach and as they joined the strangers northward in the roadway looking bleak and saying nothing, Forsythe called out to all of them.

"If you follow us now and shoot the teams or do anything else you're thinkin' of—she dies. Remember that, lawmen—she dies. And it'll be a slow death." Forsythe looked ahead and cried out: "Let her go," to the Missourian up there on his high seat.

At once the renegade-driver whistled, flicked the lines and flung off the wheel-brake. The coach jerked, rocked back and forth as the horses hit their collars, then moved out, grinding grittily over powder-fine dust.

Jared Merritt took several forward steps. From the rear window of the coach he could see Forsythe watching them. Forsythe was holding up his cocked sixgun as the coach gathered momentum on the downhill side of that little naked knoll where all this had happened.

At once Jack Carson ran to Marshal Belmont. "*Do something,*" he exclaimed. "Someone loan me a gun."

But Belmont ignored Carson. He also ignored ashen-faced old Jared and black-eyed, savage-looking Miranda, standing back there in the thin shade watching the coach rattle onward with no show of emotion in her face at all.

He went up where those bitter-eyed men were standing in the roadway and addressed the grizzled, greying man. "The extra horses we brought along are out through the trees. Go with my possemen an' get astride. Head due south and keep the coach in sight. It's got three possible courses. It can head for a local ranch for saddlehorses or it can risk going right on down into Thunder City. The least likely choice for those men is to try and get clean away using the stage. They won't do that; they'll want to get on good fast saddle animals. Follow 'em and don't get within rifle-range."

The grizzled man nodded. "And you?" he quietly asked.

"First off I'll send the girl's father, the Indian woman and their rangeboss down to town with some of the boys I brought up here with me. Whichever three of them have big, stout horses that can carry double. Then I'm going to show Forsythe what a fool move he made by not trading his hostages for those breedy fine horses his crew was riding. I'll take his big bay thoroughbred and get far down-country in front of that coach, then; whatever Forsythe does, the minute he trades the stage for saddle-horses and gets astride, I'll out-ride him and set up an ambush."

The grizzled man stood there stoically sweating, listening to all this, and when Belmont finished he said briskly, "You can't set up no ambush alone. I'll come with you."

Hyde Belmont started to shake his head. From over in the trees a Thunder City posseman called out, saying, "Marshal; you want us to fetch up the horses?" Belmont, temporarily diverted, agreed to this. He also instructed the possemen to bring up those breedy animals they'd acquired from the wild bunch. Then he turned back, but before he could speak the greying man spoke again.

"Marshal, the best intentions in this world are never

good enough," he pointed out flatly. "It's fire-power that counts." He gestured towards a lanky listening rifleman standing there at his side. "This here is my deputy from Cherokee County. He can lead our men and your posse too, just as well as either you or I can." The grizzled man didn't give Belmont a chance to protest, if that had been his intention. He turned towards his companion and issued some elemental orders. "You heard the marshal, Slim; keep 'em in sight but don't crowd 'em. They just might kill the girl. The marshal and I will get around 'em and try an ambush. You hear gunshots, you come a-runnin'. Understand?"

The lanky individual called Slim solemnly nodded. He seemed about to speak but he never got the chance because those possemen over near the trees came pushing on up into the roadway with a big band of saddled animals.

Marshal Belmont cast an experienced and admiring eye over Buck Forsythe's thousand-dollar horse. He accepted the reins, stepped over to test the cinch, dumped his carbine into Forsythe's empty saddle-boot and sprang up. He was twisting in the saddle to issue orders to the possemen when Jared reached out to touch his leg.

"Marshal; let me go with you. She's my girl. My only—"

"You're goin' back to Thunder City, Mister Merritt. So is your rangeboss and the Indian woman. You wait for us there."

Belmont motioned at some of his possemen. He

didn't allow either Jared Merritt, or Jack Carson who had just walked over, to say a thing. He explained what he had in mind and he also gave orders for Kathy's father, his rangeboss, and old Miranda the Choctaw squaw to be taken down to Thunder City. Finally, he pointed out the lanky stranger standing over there speaking back and forth with the grizzled man and said that one would now be in charge until they all met again.

Dust was hanging in the breathless overhead atmosphere as those two mounted men came together amid their anxious companions, turned, booted out their animals and went loping off southward.

CHAPTER SIXTEEN

NE thing neither the grizzled sheriff from a northward county or Hyde Belmont of Thunder City had mentioned back there in front of Jared Merritt, Jack Carson or Miranda, was what troubled Belmont most now, as he rocketed southward in the dusty wake of the stolen coach.

Those iron-bound bullion boxes in that coach had been put there deliberately; they were neither the right bullion boxes, nor were their contents valuable. Each box was filled with stones. They were heavy and they would deceive anyone until the locks were shot off and the lids thrown back.

"And that," said Belmont to the grizzled lawman, "just might be all it'll take to get her killed."

The other lawman said nothing, but he obviously had

been thinking along the same lines. They were a full mile onward coming at long last to the endless open country below Thunder Pass when he said, "Forsythe needs her more than he needs his gun an' I'm bettin' he realises it. With her dead he doesn't stand a chance."

"Small consolation," muttered Belmont, and turned to studying that tell-tale high dust-banner that lay like a dun-coloured smoke-screen straight southward in the direction of Thunder City. He and the sheriff from Cherokee County conserved their powerful animals. As long as daylight held they wouldn't have to hurry, only keep that dust-banner in sight ahead of them.

An hour later with the sun beginning to redden as it fell off westerly the sheriff said he thought Forsythe was doing the last thing he, the sheriff, would attempt, were he in Forsythe's boots.

"He's heading straight for Thunder City."

Belmont reserved judgment. He knew this country much better than did his companion. There were a number of large cow outfits roundabout; Forsythe could veer off anywhere down here and make for one of those places. He gave the outlaw leader credit for more sense than to try and bluff his way through after arriving in that aroused town down there.

And Belmont was proven correct. One mile short of Thunder City's tarpaper environs the dust-banner veered eastward. The sheriff saw this and puckered his eyes to concentrate upon it.

Belmont, with the local roundabout countryside firmly fixed in his mind, said with a hint of anticipation in his voice, "All right, Sheriff; now we know the first thing he's going to do. Off easterly there, lies the Kurt Ranch."

"And fresh saddle horses," growled the man from Cherokee County.

Belmont shook his head. "When a man has as long to think things over as I have he, at one time or another, hits upon just about every contingency that might arise. Forsythe won't find any fresh horses at the Kurt place."

The sheriff turned and stared, then quietly grunted and looked back where that dust-banner was leading them off on a tangent away from the stageroad. "You passed the word, I take it," he said.

Belmont didn't reply to this, he instead put his full attention upon their fresh destination, and the hurrying course of that fleeing stagecoach.

A little brushy hill lay ahead of them. Belmont made directly for this, angled up to its gravelly top and halted up there to blow his horse. The big bay was hardly sucking air at all. He was not only sound as new money in the wind, he was also in iron-hard good shape.

Below and perhaps two miles off lay a weathered clutch of saw-log ranch buildings. That dust-banner was speeding directly towards that ranch down there. Ahead of it, small in the distance, was the stolen coach. As Belmont and the man from Cherokee County watched, the coach spun off the eastward trail to head northward directly towards those buildings.

Belmont faintly inclined his head. He didn't say so, but so far Buck Forsythe was doing exactly what he'd thought he might do. Now came the prickly part. Would Forsythe, after determining he'd get no saddle animals at that ranch down there, return to the road and make a desperate bid to reach Thunder City and fresh horses, or would he head on eastward with the tiring coach teams? If Belmont was to get ahead for his ambush he had to guess right about this the first time.

The sheriff said, "They're stoppin' in the yard down there. I hope to hell them ranchers don't start shooting."

"They won't, Sheriff; not when they see Forsythe has Kathy Merritt."

The sheriff muttered something which Marshal Belmont ignored. Red sunlight beat mercilessly down across their backs and shoulders bringing on fresh sweat. Across the Thunder Mountains that constant blue-blurred haze was turning colour, was becoming sooty with a soft greyness that presaged dusk, but in summertime Oklahoma full night would not fall until near ten o'clock this time of year.

Belmont finally said, turning his horse back down off the hillock. "Come on, Sheriff, it's a long chance but we've got to take it."

They went southward paralleling the stageroad for a mile and halted again. Here, with the heat more intense, the Texan explained.

"He's going to figure out what I've done—stripped the local outfits of horses—and he's going to be desperate. If he goes eastward he'll know his teams are going to play out before tomorrow morning. If he turns back towards Thunder City he may believe he's got a slim chance of quitting the coach and getting horses."

"He'll sure as hell know there are horses available in

Thunder City," agreed the sheriff.

"Yeah," murmured the marshal of Thunder City. "And he'll also figure out there'll be guns waiting to kill him down there."

The grizzled sheriff wagged his head dourly. "No one's goin' to shoot him as long as he's got *her.* He'll know that, Marshal, so I'm bettin' my money he'll take the chance on Thunder City."

But Buck Forsythe did what neither of them had anticipated. He left the coach at the Kurt Ranch sitting forlornly in the yard, cut out its six horses and took enough saddles and bridles at gun-point to make his escape eastward. He also discovered, while his men were rigging out the team-animals, what was in his precious bullion boxes, but now the primary concern of Forsythe and his wild bunch was escape, not vengeance, so they put Kathy astride a big feather-legged beast with a gait like a sledgehammer and galloped on eastward with the riders of the Kurt Ranch warned against following, a warning which those people took literally but which did not prevent one of them from riding hell-for-leather down towards Thunder City.

It was from this man, as well as the unavoidable and tell-tale dustcloud, that Marshal Belmont and the sheriff of adjacent Cherokee County got their first hint of what had happened. Belmont sent the Kurt Ranch cowboy northward to search out the posse and alert it to the new direction Forsythe was taking, then those two lifted their horses over into a mile-eating lope and held them to it.

The animals had enjoyed a long rest, had their wind

150

back and were not only fresher than Forsythe's horses, but were also much speedier.

Still, with Forsythe's lead, it took nearly an hour for the pair of pursuing lawmen to get those five riders in sight, and even after they did, with the easterly broken country ahead, they were able to catch only intermittent glimpses as the outlaws raced up a hill and sped around a distant slope, and all the time the sun was dropping constantly lower in the red-chalky west.

The sheriff from Cherokee County made a cigarette as he raced along. He did this one-handed, a feat much admired among rangemen. He lit up the same way and he afterwards slowed when Belmont did to skirt along carefully over an obsidian ledge. They had closed the gap between themselves and Buck Forsythe's outlaw crew considerably and still hadn't really let their 'borrowed' horses out into a full run.

"Just a matter of time," commented the sheriff, squinting ahead and making his experienced assessments. "Just a matter of time. Marshal; just how well do you know the country east of Thunder City?"

Belmont's answer was blunt. "About as well as you do, Sheriff."

But this didn't seem to trouble the grizzled lawman at all. He booted his mount out again when they'd cleared the glass-rock ledge and went careening along behind Belmont still smoking his cigarette. He was a hard one; nothing much could disturb him. He was long-of-tooth at this lawman's game, had been in nearly every fix a gunfighter could be gotten into, and in a chase like this with the end inevitable he was concerned, not with the pursuit at all, but with the kind of country he would be shortly called upon to fight in; he had no doubt at all how this was going to end. He only had doubt about how Kathy might, or might not, survive it.

Belmont hit a long level stretch that distantly ran upwards to the top-out of a bisecting long rib of land. He gave the thoroughbred its head. In a twinkling the sheriff was spitting dust and hammering his own beast to keep up. Belmont streaked straight onward, the sheriff fell steadily farther back despite the best efforts of his gallant mount, and eventually the sheriff, realising the definite limitations of the horse he rode, ceased belabouring the animal and let it race along as best it could.

Belmont reached that top-out a full four minutes ahead of his companion. He had his first good view of the fugitives from up there. That long burst of speed had put him within a short mile of Forsythe's crew. They were galloping along without actually covering much ground. Kathy was up front between Forsythe and Frank Canton. Behind those three rode the Missourian and that younger outlaw. As the sheriff came up on his straining mount, reined down and peered ahead, Forsythe suddenly threw up an arm to halt his companions. Instantly Belmont sprang down and swung his bay horse back down behind him off the hilltop. The sheriff did the same thing. Then the pair of them dropped belly-down atop their landswell and watched.

Forsythe turned back and sat a moment studying his backtrail. Frank Canton also did this but the Missourian and his riding-pardner only cast one cursory glance rearward before dismounting to tighten cinches and gaze ruefully at the heavily muscled-up, big-boned horses they were riding. Even at that distance and in the failing light Belmont and the sheriff could surmise the expression on those two faces; after being careful to ride only the finest available horses against just exactly such a contingency as this, the Missourian and the youngest outlaw were now fleeing for their lives on horses no self-respecting cowboy would be caught dead with.

"And that," murmured the sheriff grimly, "is the way the cards fall sometimes. The best plans a man makes fall all apart. They're done for an' they know it—if there's anyone chasin' 'em."

Forsythe said something. The two dismounted men rose up over leather again and Forsythe changed course completely. Now, he was riding due south.

"Not so dumb at that," growled the sheriff, rising up to knock dry grass and dust off his clothing. "He's headin' for Thunder City this time for sure. Figures it'll be dark when he gets there; they'll be able to get good mounts in the night and be on their way."

Belmont swore as he went back to the bay horse, got astride and turned him back. The sheriff was more philosophical. As they rattled on down across a southward dry creekbed he said, "They're only puttin' it off, Marshal. They're only making their final desperate bid for freedom. They can't possibly win. To get clear they'd have to sprout wings."

Belmont had nothing to say until, with dusk at long last mantling the land with its velvet softness and its after-hours hush, they came out of the broken country and saw the stageroad lying west of them with its grey-shining twin ribbons.

He lifted his arm and pointed onward where several little orange pin-pricks of light softly shone in the shadowy evening. "Thunder City," he said, and that was all.

They had to follow Forsythe now almost entirely by sound, which meant they'd stop every thousand yards or so and pick up the solid beat of shod hooves striking hard down over summertime iron-hard soil. If Forsythe had also stopped they could easily have lost him now, and realising this they pushed up recklessly to get close enough to perhaps spy that hard-riding bunched-up group of renegades. They couldn't actually make the wild bunch out until, within a mile of Thunder City, town lights occasionally winked out as horsemen passed between the two lawmen and the onward lights. This gave them as much as they needed even though it never did permit them a clear sighting of their enemies.

Belmont hauled down to let the sheriff come up close beside him. "It's dark enough now so they just might get away with it, Sheriff, especially since no one'll be really expectin' them like this."

"Where'll they head for?"

Belmont had his answer ready. "My guess is that a couple of them will head for the liverybarn up here at the north end of town, and the others will scatter out to stand ready where they hid their dynamite-bombs."

The sheriff's eyes flew wide open. "Dynamite-bombs?" he gasped. "What—?"

"I'll explain about that later. Right now there's nothing to worry about. We've already found the bombs and taken them away. Now listen close, Sheriff; if that's what they do we can take the ones at the liverybarn—with a lot of luck—because they'll be split up."

"But hell—what about the girl?"

Belmont was dismounting when he said, "Come on. Leave your horse where I leave mine. Never mind the Winchester. From here on this'll be sixgun work. Katherine?" Belmont strode ahead. "I don't know. That's our only big worry right now."

"Yeah," mumbled the sheriff. "That—and stayin' alive."

They didn't enter Thunder City by the main roadway, but passed shadowily out and around to strike a north-south alleyway and enter over there. They left their horses tied to an ancient tree and walked through thickening gloom, one behind the other, Hyde Belmont in the lead.

CHAPTER SEVENTEEN

THE Texan had made a good guess. He knew it the second he flattened outside the liverybarn with the sheriff of Cherokee County beside him. From up inside the barn near the poorly-lighted roadway entrance men's voices sounded deep and low.

"You just mind your manners old man and no one gets hurt. You get to thinkin' heroic thoughts and you'll be the deadest damned hero west of the Missouri."

Belmont rolled his head sideways. "Canton," he breathed. "I was hoping he'd be the one to go hunt up their cussed bombs."

Another voice spoke out, up there. It said in a sharp and

recognisable manner. "Which are your fastest horses, old-timer, and be quick now."

That was Buck Forsythe himself. The answer was too low and mumbled for Belmont to make it out. He dropped low and risked a peek inside where a smoky coal-oil lamp spluttered from a nail near the barn's office doorway. He saw Canton, Forsythe, and Katherine Merritt up there. Katherine was sitting slumped in an old battered chair by that office door.

Belmont drew back. It crossed his mind that with luck he could apprehend the youngest outlaw and the perpetually grinning Missourian, but he didn't want to leave this spot. Not for as long as Kathy was up there.

He considered slipping inside the barn but abandoned that notion the moment one of those armed men began walking back towards the rear alley. He and the sheriff sidled swiftly on across where a dilapidated old shed stood, stepped into gloomy darkness back out of sight and kept an intent watch ahead.

Frank Canton appeared in the alleyway opening. He still had his carbine. He balanced there looking right and left, testing the night and listening to all the small sounds of Thunder City after nightfall. Evidently nothing alerted him to danger for he suddenly turned and walked back up where he'd left Forsythe and the liveryman.

The sheriff and Thunder City's marshal had an excellent view. Kathy showed as a dejected silhouette up there beneath that smoking old lantern. Forsythe and the liveryman went across to the easternmost rank of tie-stalls, evidently to select the horses, and Frank Canton paced on up to lean with deceptive but hard-eyed vigilance upon a doorjamb where he commanded a good view of the main roadway. Hyde Belmont saw all this and kept forming plans and discarding them until he finally turned and said, "You watch this back-alley. Those other two are going to discover we've already removed their bombs. The minute they realise they don't have any whip-hand they're going to rush back here to warn Forsythe."

"I'll take care of 'em," growled the tough-faced sheriff. "Where you goin'?"

"Inside the barn."

"*What!* If they see you they'll—"

"It's now or never," snapped Belmont. "If I can get the girl out of the way we'll have them."

"Maybe you'd better just sit tight a few minutes. The posse'll be ridin' in."

"I know that, Sheriff, and that's exactly why I want to try and get her out of there first, if I can, because the minute Canton sees a big body of horsemen enter town he's going to know she's their last chance."

Belmont slipped away, crossed the dark alley and dropped low over by the barn's rear entrance. He could hear men moving around in there, could hear horses also moving. Evidently Forsythe had made his selection of the animals they meant to continue their flight upon.

But Belmont had to wait until Forsythe and the liveryman led all those animals up near the office door before he could safely jump inside, keep those bunched-up horses between himself and the onward men, whip around to his right and drop down behind a tie-stall partition. While he was crouched there he heard Forsythe turn and call out to Frank Canton asking whether Canton had seen their other two men yet. Frank replied that he had not. Then he said something that made Belmont believe somewhere along the escape trail Canton had become critical of Forsythe. He said, "We'll make it now; you can quit worryin', Buck. Between the girl and the bombs isn't no one goin' to jump us. But if you just aren't happy unless you're worryin'—why then—worry about how you're goin' to live down lettin' those tin-star lawmen make a monkey out of you all around."

Forsythe said something coldly back to Canton but Belmont, with his head half beyond the tie-stall partition straining to make out Katherine Merritt up there, paid Forsythe no more attention.

Belmont had ducked into and out of three more in-line tie-stalls; he was within a short stones'-throw of Buck Forsythe's back where the outlaw leader and the badly shaken liveryman were rigging out those horses. He saw Kathy lift her head and turn it directly towards him almost as though she knew he was there. He froze until she swung the other way to consider Canton where he lounged in the doorway, a smoking cigarette drooping from his lipless mouth, his Winchester carbine grounded in front of him.

Belmont could have gotten the drop on both those renegades then and there but he feared risking it. He instead worked around one more tie-stall—this one with a fat big mare in it—and was at long last only about eight feet from Kathy.

But that final eight feet might just as well have been eighty feet because, the moment he moved out of the fat mare's stall he would no longer have any concealment at all; Forsythe would see him, couldn't help but see him because Buck was facing towards the office wall as he saddled up one of those patient-standing livery horses out there in the gloomy runway.

Frank Canton turned, squinted down into the barn and said, "What the hell's keepin' 'em?" He sounded irritated more than apprehensive. He'd obviously meant the other two outlaws.

Forsythe finished his second animal, gave the latigo a little tug and stepped over to the last unsaddled horse as he said, a trifle stiffly as though he was thinking unkind thoughts about Frank Canton, "You just keep watch out there. They'll be along as soon as they've lit those fuses."

"That's what's botherin' me," growled Canton. "Damned if I want to be within a country mile of this stinking cow-town when all that powder goes off."

Forsythe lifted his head and peered out through the roadway opening. He seemed to Marshal Belmont to be trying to estimate how much time had elapsed since the band of them had gotten into town. In the end Forsythe gave his big shoulders a little shrug and stooped to pick up a saddleblanket and fling it across a horse's ready back.

Frank Canton, up in the roadway opening, spat out his smoke, clasped both hands across the muzzle of his Winchester and resumed his vigil. But Canton's profile, what Belmont could see of it in the yellow roadway reflections, was set in a tough and constant scowl now. For a change it was Canton who was being troubled by second-thoughts now, not Buck Forsythe.

Out back in the alleyway there occurred a series of sharp sounds which put Belmont's nerves instantly on edge. But at that precise moment Frank Canton turned to say, "Buck; they been gone long enough. I'm beginnin' to worry a little about 'em."

Marshal Belmont scarcely breathed as those sounds out back were caught by the liveryman, who straightened partially around over where he was adjusting the cheek-piece of a bridle, to peer down through the yonder gloom. Belmont prayed for the other two not to notice. He thought he knew what had happened out there. The sheriff of Cherokee County had jumped one, or perhaps both, of the returning outlaws.

But Forsythe answered Canton and his rumbling deep voice drowned out those lesser sounds behind the liveryman. "All right," Forsythe said crisply. "You and I'll head on out with the girl."

Canton though appeared not quite ready for this drastic move, so he squared back around and swung his head back and forth making a long, very careful survey of the yonder night-shrouded roadway.

Belmont felt sweat running into his eyes although it was not hot now. He squeezed the perspiration off with a dirty sleeve and let his breath out in a long, silent sigh.

Around them Thunder City's usual night-life made its customary sounds, sometimes loud, sometimes not too loud. Cowboys in from the ranges rode back and forth occasionally hailing one another, sometimes spurring recklessly through town in liquored-up exuberance.

Music came faintly from the saloons, men laughed

loudly out in the roadway or up along the plankwalks. Where lamplight tumbled past squared windows patches of brightness lay like orange pools in the otherwise darkened roadway.

Belmont let all this come and go without particularly heeding it. He crouched there in the unfragrant gloom beside the big fat mare who was stolidly munching her hay until his leg-muscles ached from his unnatural position, then he inched backwards to the edge of that cribbed manger behind him, groped for the mare's tie-rope and cautiously worked the bowline-knot loose. The mare went on eating. She was old and placid and wise to the peculiarities of men; if a man chose to squat there beside her smelling powerfully of sweat and anxiety, she could be entirely philosophical about it. At least until the man put a steady backward pressure upon her rope. Then she took several reluctant rearward steps.

Belmont had made an estimate of the time; had come to a hard decision. Very shortly now the possemen would inevitably be riding into town. If he didn't have Katherine Merritt clear of harm's way by then, the chances were better than even that Frank Canton or Buck Forsythe would kill her, because obviously, the moment the cry was raised that Forsythe was here in their town, the cowboys and townsmen would attack them, ignorant of the fact that the moment they opened fire Katherine Merritt would die.

He backed the fat old mare steadily out into the rearward runway. She went without much coaxing although she showed absolutely no enthusiasm at being compelled to leave her big bait of hay. When she cleared the tie-stall Belmont took his big gamble; he raised up just enough to swing her off to his right, swing her hindquarters up towards Forsythe so that she was backing between the outlaw chieftain and Kathy, who was still over there on that rickety old barn-chair.

Again, it wasn't either of the occupied outlaws who saw this new presence, it was the liveryman. He finished with the horse's bridle he'd been adjusting, turned and growled at the old mare.

"Consarn you, Sadie, where you figure you're goin'?"

He stepped carefully forward to catch that hanging lead-shank, moved slowly so as not to startle the old mare. He turned as Buck Forsythe swung to frown over at him. He mumbled apologetically that the old mare had worked herself loose; that she was a wise old critter and that he'd tie her up again.

Forsythe had the reins of all three saddled horses in his hands. Belmont saw this. He also saw the liveryman's hatted head bobbing across the big mare's round withers and stepped fully ahead, bent, caught hold of Kathy's arm and gave her a quick, violent pull up out of the chair. She whipped upright and half around facing Belmont, her mouth open to cry out, her eyes nearly black with quick, sharp astonishment. She was yanked in behind the old mare out of Buck Forsythe's sight. At about the same time the liveryman stepped up, caught the mare's dangling rope—and saw Marshal Belmont with Katherine Merritt back there on the mare's off-side. His jaw dropped.

Belmont's grip on Kathy's wrist was like iron. She

fought down a moan of anguish as he wrenched her ten feet westward to an empty tie-stall, flung her back in there and dropped to one knee as he drew his sixgun.

"Well," barked Forsythe at the stunned liveryman. "Tie the damned mare back in her stall. Don't just stand there! Hey, Frank, we better get out of here. So far it's quiet. If we wait any longer something's going to bust wide open sure as hell."

Canton turned inward, ranged his eyes over the horses and said, "If they been caught, Buck, there could be an ambush set up."

Forsythe ran this possibility through his mind and said, "Come on; we can still make it as long as we put the girl out front."

Canton turned completely around. "What's that damned liveryman doing in there with that fat mare?" he sharply demanded.

"She worked loose. He's re-tying her. Frank, take one more look up an' down the roadway."

Canton obediently turned and looked, stood for nearly fifteen seconds considering every strolling figure along the plankwalks. "Nothing," he growled. "No sight of them, Buck. I'm gettin' a bad feeling. They been took sure as hell." Canton hoisted his carbine, turned and walked on over to the nearest saddled horse, up-ended his carbine to drop it into the saddle-boot, and froze like that, his carbine wrong-ended in the air and perfectly still. Canton was staring around his mount's head at the empty chair where Katherine Merritt had been.

In a very calm, deliberate tone he said, "Buck, where's the girl?"

Forsythe whipped around, sprang out from around a horse and halted stock-still, also staring at that chair. He suddenly spun half around and made a lunge towards the old liveryman, his gun-hand dropping in a blur. "Damn you, what've you done with her?" he roared.

The old liveryman, caught not entirely by surprise but paralysed by fear as Forsythe's sixgun swooped upwards and stopped dead-level with his middle, croaked waveringly, "Mister, I didn't—I don't know—what 'come of her. She was right in that chair last time I—"

Frank Canton broke through that quavering voice saying, "She's hidin' in one of the stalls, Buck. Fan out. You take that side, I'll take the north side."

Canton was moving as he said this. He was several feet away from the horses when Belmont got a good sighting. But it was the old liveryman's terrified scream: *"Don't— please don't!"* that brought Belmont's head whipping around.

Forsythe was cocking his sixgun; his pale-lighted face was closed down and completely merciless. Belmont had no time to think about the peril of his own position, with Frank Canton nearly abreast of the tie-stall where he and Kathy crouched in ammonia-scented blackness.

Belmont fired.

That thunderous explosion lit up the barn with a crimson, blinding flash of muzzleblast-light. The noise was deafening in this confined place. Buck Forsythe went drunkenly backwards, his gun-arm flung half around as momentum propelled him rearward.

Forsythe's hair-triggered .45 detonated from spasmodic reflex as the outlaw leader convulsed, bent far over forward as though to protect his soft parts from the next bullet.

Those startled horses panicked, flung around in the tight place where they'd stood, and two of them ran straight out into the yonder roadway while the other two went in the opposite direction. It was one of these animals that struck Forsythe a violent blow knocking him down. The second horse charged right up over the writhing outlaw, his steel-shod hooves inexorably grinding Forsythe's dwindling life out of him.

Somewhere northward on up the roadway a man cried out in sudden, high-pitched alarm. Belmont heard that outcry as he fell back and rolled clear, one half a second ahead of Frank Canton's searching gunshot, and Canton's snarled outcry of astonishment, wrath, and deadly intent.

Kathy's softness stopped Marshal Belmont. He reached out to fling her down flat, raised up and thumbed off two fast shots towards Canton's muzzle-blast over across the way.

CHAPTER EIGHTEEN

OMEWHERE out in the back alley a bull-bass voice cried out indistinguishably just a moment ahead of Marshal Belmont's two shots, and after them, other men's sharp cries rang out around front where most of Thunder City's saloons stood.

The liveryman was suddenly nowhere to be seen. That

big old fat mare set back on her tie-rope but couldn't break free.

Belmont was desperate. Frank Canton was the most deadly of defunct Buck Forsythe's wild bunch, was somewhere over across the runway from him and now the liverybarn was plunged into solid darkness. Canton had deliberately shot out that coal-oil lantern hanging up there near the office doorway, the barn was steeped in an endless darkness. Belmont groped for Kathy, found her and pulled himself inch by silent inch upwards until he lay directly in front of her. His body protected her.

A terrifying minute of total hush drew out inside the barn, while outside, in back as well as out front, men's cries and shouts of alarm as well as of warning, made the yonder night seem peopled by dozens of wary spectators.

A body of horsemen came down into town from the northward darkness. Their sounds were loud in the night as they called forth asking quick questions and getting back quick answers.

Marshal Belmont felt in his belt-loops for three fresh loads. He used this precious respite to re-load in, and afterwards he rolled his head around until he could vaguely make out the pale blur of Katherine Merritt's face. She was straining out across the barn where Canton was. She put her lips to Belmont's ear and whispered.

"He moved southward. I saw him run on down there when you fired those two shots."

Belmont nodded and crept away, crept on up to the

very edge of that heavy partitioning planking which separated each tie-stall from the stall next to it. There, he got flat-down and pushed his gun-hand forward. From the right-hand edge of his vision Belmont could see shadows moving warily out in the yonder roadway. He did not let these silhouettes distract him as he considered it probable that Frank Canton was striving to reach the back-alley.

Out of pure instinct he said, "Canton; forget it. The alley's no way out for you."

The smashing gunshot he got back from Canton warned him about trying to reason with the gunman again. That bullet had splintered the heavy plank above his head.

He risked a reckless southward shot, heard his slug tear through wood splintering it, and also heard a frantic sound as someone with spurs on their boots jumped away from that shot. He fired again, this time aiming in a general fashion still farther down the barn. This time though, he heard nothing, and assumed that his shot hadn't been close at all.

It was when he fired his third shot over across the runway that it came to him what Canton was probably attempting. The killer knew he couldn't shoot his way out through the front roadway. He also knew by now he couldn't fight his way out through the back alley. That left wily Frank Canton only one solid alternative: *He had to get back his hostage!*

Belmont risked a look out and around his tie-stall partition. If Canton had crossed to his side of the barn he could be slipping up on Belmont and Kathy right this moment. But there was nothing to see, and because of the noise outside the barn, there was nothing to be heard either.

Marshal Belmont sucked back, got both legs gathered up under him and began to slowly raise up. He stopped just short of the partition's top-out, raised his .45 and fired overhand and downward. Someone let off a sharp bleat of alarm and astonishment out behind the barn. Evidently that blind shot had scattered some too-close spectators.

But it also accomplished something else, for Canton *was* across the runway working his way up towards Belmont's stall, and when he fired right back Marshal Belmont had his solid proof of this.

He turned, took two large steps, caught Kathy by the arm and drew her forward. He meant to ease her around into the next stall eastward out of harm's way, but as he tried to go forward with her Canton let go with two hard-driving slugs that splintered one of the partitioning wall's heavy planks driving both Marshal Belmont and Kathy Merritt flat down.

Belmont did not fire back. He lay there furiously shucking out spent casings from his sixgun and pushing in fresh loads. Afterwards he put his mouth to Kathy's ear and desperately told her to get around into the next stall. She listened but made no move to obey and Marshal Belmont had no time to argue with her because Canton drove another slug into—and through—that broken stretch of tie-stall-siding. Canton knew exactly what he was doing. He was coldly practical; no amount of chaos seemed to rattle him in the least. He clearly meant to batter down that broken board then finish off Belmont and regain his hostage.

Out in the front roadway old Jared Merritt's unmistakable voice cried out for men to rush the barn. Another recognisable voice, that of Jack Carson, just as loudly warned the cowboys and crowding-up townsmen out there not to attempt anything so suicidal.

From out back the rough, profane voice of the Cherokee County sheriff ordered the men to tighten their surround of the barn. This same voice informed everyone within hearing distance that he'd already captured two of the outlaws, and had also seen Buck Forsythe get shot down. In conclusion he roared: "There's only Frank Canton left out of the wild bunch, boys, but Canton's the worst of the lot. Don't any of you try slippin' in there to try helpin' Marshal Belmont because if Canton don't drill you Belmont might. Just tighten the surround and wait—and pray."

For a space of several minutes after the sheriff ceased yelling, there wasn't a sound anywhere. Marshal Belmont turned to order Kathy on out of the stall again. He'd just begun to speak when Canton, who had evidently taken this time to re-load, fired another bullet through that splintered plank. Both Marshal Belmont and Kathy dropped back down, their faces in pungent straw bedding.

Belmont gave up trying to coax Kathy to move, turned, took long aim through the shattered planking and fired. He waited several seconds and fired again. He did this four times, then, confident he'd driven Canton down while Frank waited for that fifth and sixth shot, Belmont caught Kathy's arm and sprang upright dragging her along and whipped around into the next stall where he instantly dropped down and forced Kathy down also.

Canton, hearing the slam of booted feet and understanding how he'd been fooled, roared out an ugly curse and fired twice more through that broken siding into the empty tie-stall.

Belmont crouched there re-loading. Sweat ran under his clothing in rivulets, ran into his eyes until he pushed it away with a sleeve and closed the gate on his re-charged weapon.

A sudden strange sound somewhere inside the barn with the three of them caught Marshal Belmont's attention and held it. It was a trilling sort of little cry that an injured bird might make and try as he might Belmont could not make out the direction that cry was coming from.

Kathy suddenly sprang up to her knees and threw forth a hand to grip Belmont's gun-arm. "Miranda," she whispered in a breathless way. "Miranda's in here with us somewhere."

Belmont looked around puzzled. Kathy peered up close into his face and nodded.

That peculiar trilling sound came again. Frank Canton suddenly cursed and fired two quick, random shots around into the darkness. The trilling sounded temporarily stopped, then as the echoes of those shots died away, began again, only it grew louder, more insistent. It sounded like the directionless steady throbbing sound of a huge cricket.

Out in the roadway Jack Carson also recognised the sound and cried out to Jared. There were others who also knew that sound, for these were all Oklahomans, born and raised in the Indian Nations. Frank Canton was one of them. He roared curses and slammed wild shots around him.

Marshal Belmont and Katherine Merritt were still as stone. For Belmont, who knew the Indian ways, this echoless trilling was the warning, the alarm. He was awaiting what came next.

And it came, suddenly and harshly, the guttural gobble of a fighting turkey rooster—the Indian call to fight!

This time Frank Canton's un-strung nerves gave way. He sprang up and emptied his sixgun towards the more readily placed sound of that turkey gobbling. He afterwards, with Marshal Belmont and Kathy watching fascinated, stepped one full step forward and hurled his empty gun over into the yonder darkness. Canton had seen something over there no one else saw. He abruptly gave a choked-off sob and staggered backwards, both hands flying upwards to his chest. Belmont and Kathy had heard nothing, seen nothing, but they made out the professional killer's unsteady waverings.

Marshal Belmont stepped out, lifted his cocked .45 and strode ahead. Canton saw him coming; he tried to turn his right hand outward but the movement was awkward, as though his muscles were turning flaccid. Belmont stepped up to strike aside Canton's sixgun and Frank dropped the weapon, lifted a stricken face, and collapsed.

There was a hardwood-handled skinning-knife protruding from his chest with only the handle and two inches of steel visible. Canton fell forward onto his knees. He died hard. He fought to get back upright, couldn't, and put out one hand to hold himself off the runway floor. But he failed here too and fell with a soft rustling sound at Belmont's feet.

Somewhere behind the marshal Kathy's sharp outcry resounded as she ran headlong on across into an opposite tie-stall and dropped to her knees over there murmuring a name over and over.

"Miranda, Miranda . . ."

Men called inquiringly from out back and out front. Belmont didn't heed them. He got down on one knee beside Frank Canton, rolled him over onto his back and traded stares with the swiftly failing killer. There was no pity, no compassion, passing back and forth between these two. Each of them despised everything the other stood for. Canton closed his dulling eyes and gave a little jerky, bubbly cough, and died.

Belmont considered that hard-handled knife briefly, got up and walked over where Kathy was cradling Miranda's head in her lap. She looked up, her eyes stricken.

"She's dead, Marshal. Miranda's dead."

He considered that grim, dark face, all loose and relaxed now as though in deep sleep, and gently nodded. "They have a saying among the Choctaw, Kathy: There is a good time to die and a bad time to die. Miranda knew the good time." He bent and lifted her. "Come," he softly said, and led her out through the runway down to the back-alley where men rushed forward, foremost among them the sheriff from Cherokee County.

"You got him!" exulted the grizzled, tough old greying lawman.

The Texan shook his head. "Go in there and look. Miranda the Indian woman got him—eight inches of skinning-knife-steel half through his chest."

They paced away from those excited men, went on down to a crossroads and turned to pass on up the main roadway.

Kathy walked as though in a trance. She didn't look up until old Jared and Jack Carson spied them walking along and came running.

"Miranda's dead," she said lifelessly. "Canton shot her in the barn."

Jared was shocked. "Miranda? Why honey—she was out here with us. She came back with us ridin' double."

Hyde Belmont had a supporting arm around Kathy's waist. He looked over her shoulder at those two stunned, white faces. "It's true," he said quietly. "Miranda got inside the barn, drew Canton's attention off us, and when he turned towards her she threw a knife. His shot killed her but that skinning-knife killed Canton."

Jared reached for his daughter with both arms. She looked over at him and the scalding dry-hot tears finally came. But she didn't cry aloud. It was worse for those three exhausted, drained-dry men to see the racking sobs tear at her through bottomless, totally silent anguish.

Jared took her into his arms and held her close while Carson and Marshal Belmont walked discreetly away. Half the men in Thunder City were crowding into the shot-up liverybarn, few had eyes for those two tall men walking along northward through the pleasant, quiet night.

"I had no idea she'd do that," Marshal Belmont said finally.

Carson nodded understandingly, but he knew a lot more about Miranda the Choctaw than Hyde Belmont did. "I'll tell you how it was," he said softly. "Kathy was her idol. I've seen her ready to kill men before when they only smiled at Katherine. Miranda knew only one love and one loyalty, and those fools in the barn made the worst possible mistake when they took Kathy with them. Miranda would have followed them to the end of the earth—on her hands and knees if necessary—but she'd never have gone to her grave without settling with them. That's the way she was from the first day Jared brought her to the ranch. She was more than Kathy's companion; she was also her watchdog."

"Then," exclaimed Belmont, coming to a halt up beyond the sounds of the crowd in the liverybarn, "I reckon that's the way she wanted it, Carson."

"It is, Marshal. Believe me, that's exactly the way she wanted it."

Carson pushed out his grimy, raw-knuckled hand. "We're plumb obliged to you, Marshal. As for Kathy . . ."

"Yes?"

Carson pumped Hyde Belmont's big hand and dropped it. "Drop by the ranch in a week or so, Marshal. I've known her since she was a little girl too. She'll be right glad to see you again."

Marshal Belmont's tired eyes lighted a little and his lips curled pleasantly upwards at their outer corners. "I'll do that, Jack. I give you my word—I'll do that."

Center Point Publishing
600 Brooks Road • PO Box 1
Thorndike ME 04986-0001 USA

(207) 568-3717

US & Canada:
1 800 929-9108